A TIME TO REAP

April, 1963: Widowed two years previously, and with two small daughters, Elizabeth Duncan surprised everyone by taking on the position of farm manager at the Rosland estate, left vacant when her husband died. This winter has been hard, but Elizabeth is doing well — despite the fact that someone seems to be trying to sabotage her. A new relationship is the last thing on her mind. However, as she dances at the annual estate ball, that may be about to change . . .

KATE BLACKADDER

A TIME TO REAP

Complete and Unabridged

LINFORD
Leicester

First published in Great Britain in 2016

First Linford Edition
published 2017

A catalogue record for this book is available
from the British Library.

ISBN 978–1–4448–3290–7

Published by
F. A. Thorpe (Publishing)
Anstey, Leicestershire

Set by Words & Graphics Ltd.
Anstey, Leicestershire
Printed and bound in Great Britain by
T. J. International Ltd., Padstow, Cornwall

This book is printed on acid-free paper

1

'Exactly how many lambs did you lose, Mrs Duncan?' Rodney Shaw put his elbows on his desk and tapped his fingertips together as he glared at the farm manager through his horn-rimmed glasses.

Elizabeth Duncan was used to the estate factor's glare and his barked questions, and was no longer intimidated by them. She'd ignored his imperious gesture inviting her to sit down, and drew herself up to her full height — three inches taller than him even when they were both standing — and looked him in the eye as she answered.

'Ten,' she said. 'We've been luckier than most. We were able to get the sheep off the hill in time, and our fields are comparatively sheltered. But they're saying it was the coldest winter for two hundred — '

'I'm aware of that, of course. But luck shouldn't have anything to do with it.'

'Down south, hundreds have died because the lambing is a couple of months earlier than ours.' Elizabeth kept her voice calm. 'Of course I wish we hadn't lost any, but it was unavoidable.' She shuddered as she remembered the worst morning, when she'd found six sad little bodies frozen beside their puzzled mothers after a night when the temperature had plunged to minus fifteen.

'If you say so.' Rodney Shaw's tone implied that Elizabeth, and Elizabeth alone, was responsible for the icy weather that had brought the whole country to a virtual standstill for almost three months. He gestured at the piece of paper she held. 'Is that the final cost for the feed?'

Elizabeth handed it to him. The factor glanced at it and shook his head. 'Feed merchant taking advantage of the situation, it would seem. I don't know what Lady Annabel's going to say.' He waved his hand again, this time indicating that he was finished with her.

Elizabeth marched back to her own small office. Lady Annabel would have the sense to realise that there was no option but to buy extra feed when the hills were under several feet of snow, she fumed. The feed merchant had a hard job keeping up with demand. He could have charged twice as much, as they were all so desperate, but he didn't.

The snow might have disappeared from the ground, if not from the hills, but the cubbyhole at the back of the estate office building was still freezing. Elizabeth lit the paraffin heater, although she knew she wouldn't be sitting down for long, poured herself a cup of tea from the flask Tibbie had filled for her, and opened the packet of sandwiches.

The farm diary for 1963 lay open on the desk. The first of April. She should be planning when to plant the potatoes this month, but the ground was still so hard. To keep the farmhands busy today, she'd set them to do some fencing repairs and tidy the barn.

Tam, the new dairyman, had started this morning. He was due to come to the office in ten minutes, and together they were going out to look at the herd. Elizabeth hoped he and his wife and their new baby would settle in well at Rosland Farm. It was a small community, and mostly a harmonious one. Unfortunately, Tam's wife would likely find her next-door neighbour to be less than congenial.

Tam seemed to be a good person to have around, respectful but not afraid to say what he thought, his honest blue eyes twinkling with humour. Elizabeth had taken his personality into account almost as much as his dairy experience when she'd offered him the job. Mr Shaw had wanted someone else, but she hadn't taken to that hard, unsmiling man at all. It was as if *he'd* been interviewing *her* rather than the other way round. During the tour of the dairy, he'd snapped questions at her and pulled a face when she answered, evidently finding it hard to believe that a mere woman was the farm manager. Too much like Mr Shaw himself. Fortunately, Lady Annabel had made it clear that the final decision was to be Elizabeth's.

4

Tam's wife hadn't come to the interview — the journey up north from Ayrshire was tricky in the snowy weather. But Tam assured Elizabeth that she would be delighted with the semi-detached cottage that would be their new home.

She finished her ham sandwich, then folded up the brown paper bag and put it in the drawer, hoping she'd remember to take it home at the end of the day. Tibbie put on a martyred air if she forgot, and much of Elizabeth's energy went into trying to keep on her mother-in-law's good side.

Inside the drawer was a photograph of Matthew taken on their wedding day. He'd never looked quite comfortable in a suit — a check shirt with the sleeves rolled up and his old corduroys were more his style. Why was it that pictures only seemed to be taken on formal occasions? She didn't have a picture of him at work, except in her head, and she was beginning to be afraid that that picture was fading.

She used to look at the picture and ask his advice all the time — not that she would tell anyone that; they would think she was mad. But when she took over his job after the accident, she would often take him out of the drawer and quietly tell him whatever problem she was grappling with. More often than not, the solution would come to her. Now that, unbelievably, two whole years had passed, she was consulting him less, confident in her own abilities to sort things out. But knowing the picture was there gave her strength.

What on earth was that sound from next door? Rodney Shaw laughing? Surely not. She got up and looked along the corridor to his room. Jimmie Bruce, one of the farmhands, was standing in the doorway to the factor's office, twisting his cap in his hands and looking upset. He was a sweet-natured man who had never quite grown up, but he was strong as a horse, a hard worker, and a valued member of her staff.

'Jimmie?' She hurried over to him. 'Is something wrong?'

'M-Mrs Duncan — '

Before Jimmie could say any more, Rodney Shaw said: 'Just my little joke, Mrs Duncan. I sent Bruce to the shop for a tin of tartan paint, but apparently they didn't have any!' He came round his desk. 'You can get back to work now, Bruce.' He closed his door.

'Never mind Mr Shaw, Jimmie.' Elizabeth gripped the man's arm for a moment. 'He has a very warped sense of humour.' She castigated herself for not remembering that this had happened last year — then it had been 'a jar of elbow grease' that Jimmie was supposed to pick up. She held out her watch to show him the time. 'Look, it's after midday. April Fools jokes don't count now. Go and have your sandwiches. I'll come and see you later.'

It was unforgivable of the factor to make fun of poor Jimmie. Last year Elizabeth had tried to remonstrate with him about it, but he'd brushed her off. And he'd undermined her today, too, by taking the farmhand away from work she'd set him.

Was that Tam coming in now? She took a deep breath to compose herself to greet him. 'Tam. I hope you've enjoyed your first morning at Rosland.' She turned off the heater and put on her jacket. 'And I hope your wife — June, isn't it? — is getting settled in. Moving house so soon after having a baby ... If she needs any help, do ask. I'll go down and see her later.'

'Thanks, Mrs Duncan,' Tam Morrison said cheerfully. 'Sadie had us up before the birds this morning, so we cracked on with getting unpacked.'

'Good,' Elizabeth said. 'Right, let's show you round.'

2

June pinned the last nappy to the line, then picked up the laundry basket and looked up at the sky. It was so clear and blue, and the air was definitely warmer. Spring was here at long last. This was such a beautiful place. On Sunday afternoon they'd pushed the pram around the estate, with its hedged fields, and woods with the trees just coming into bud. Tam had pointed out Mrs Duncan's house and the lodge at the end of the drive where Mr Shaw lived. They'd peered through the gates of Rosland House, a grand Victorian building. It was empty most of the year, which didn't seem right, but Tam said that the estate owner, Lady Annabel, lived most of the time somewhere in England.

She turned her gaze, with joy, on the pram by the back door. After five long years they had a baby. It was a miracle — well, a miracle for Tam and herself of course, not for Rita. She could never forget Sadie's birth mother even though she desperately wanted to. Circled on the calendar and engraved on her heart was the date 17 June 1963. On that day, she hoped and prayed, Sadie would really and truly be their very own daughter.

There was another black cloud on her happiness, but this lovely morning she was not going to let her new neighbour get her down.

She hadn't ventured far on her own yet, so today she'd decided she was going to walk the mile to the village post office to buy stamps. She'd written a long letter to her mother, wishing that they had a camera to take a picture of the baby to send with it.

★   ★   ★

Nancy Douglas looked up as the bell jangled and a woman came in backwards pulling a pram. She dashed round the counter to help with the door. Luckily there were no other customers, or it

10

would be rather a squash. The pram would have been quite safe outside, but — she peered into it — this was a very new baby, and first-time mothers could be overly protective.

'How are you liking Rosland, Mrs Morrison?' she asked, enjoying the look of surprise on the newcomer's face at the use of her name.

'I'm liking it fine,' she said. 'How do you … ?'

'It wasn't difficult. I'm Nancy. I've been working in this post office for almost forty years. There's not much gets past me.'

June held out her hand. 'Nancy, nice to meet you. I'm June. And this is Sadie.' She stroked the little hand lying on the knitted blanket.

'A redhead by the look of it.' Nancy glanced at June's dark curls.

'There's red hair on my husband's side of the family,' June said almost defensively. 'I'd like six threepenny stamps, please.' She looked around with interest. The post office took up a corner of the

11

shop, which was otherwise crammed with tins and packets and all manner of household items. 'Is this where the grocery van comes from?

'Yes, it goes round all the farms and outlying areas,' said Nancy. 'Tuesday is Rosland day. Elizabeth will have told you about it. Mrs Duncan,' she added, seeing the question in June's eyes.

'She's very nice, Mrs Duncan, isn't she,' June said, sitting down on the chair Nancy kept by the counter to encourage folk to sit and chat. 'She put some food in the larder and had the fire lit for us when we arrived. It was a cheery sight. But I've never heard of a woman being a farm manager before.'

'And a good job she's making of it. I've known Elizabeth all her life.' Nancy took the money for the stamps and held out her hand for June's letter. 'I'll put it in the bag for you.' She dropped it into the sack behind the counter, glancing quickly at the address first. Paisley. Not that she was being nosy. Just gathering information.

She perched on her own chair and leaned forward on her elbows. 'Yes, I minded Elizabeth when she was a wee thing tramping around in her Wellington boots after her dad — he was a shepherd up Helmsdale way. And then in the war, when the Land Girls were here, that was it. She knew girls could be farmers too.'

'And what happened ... ?' June stopped.

Nancy beamed at her. It was natural to want to know about Elizabeth's situation, which was an unusual one, but she liked it that June had some delicacy in the asking. Then she stopped smiling as she said: 'It was terrible, terrible. Two years ago. Matthew was on his horse on the road between here and the farm. Something caused the animal to shy, and he was thrown off. The doctor came quick as he could, but it was too late. And there was Elizabeth left with the wee ones.'

'Two girls? I've seen them playing around the farmhouse.'

'Libby and Flora. Well, Elizabeth had been at the agricultural college too — that

13

was where she met Matthew — so she was well up on it all, and she begged Lady Annabel to give her a chance and let her have Matthew's job. Mr Rodney Shaw was none too pleased about it — he had a pal all lined up — but she's a very sensible woman, Lady Annabel. She could see what Elizabeth was like.'

'But how does she manage, with the children?' June was frankly curious now.

'Tibbie, Matthew's mother, moved in with her. She lost her own man in the war, and Matthew was her one and only.'

June raised her eyebrows. 'I'm awful fond of Tam's mum,' she laughed, 'but I don't think we'd get on in the same house.'

'Tibbie's not an easy woman to live with, but her heart's in the right place.' Nancy put the big book of stamps in the drawer and looked June straight in the eye. 'And what has Isa been telling you about us all?' If Nancy knew June's next-door neighbour, it would be plenty.

'Oh! She ... ' June fumbled for words.

'Let me guess.' Nancy counted on her

fingers. 'One: Nancy Douglas in the post office is an old besom who can't mind her own business. Two: she knows — did she tap the side of her nose when she said this? — who Matthew Duncan visited the afternoon he died. Three: Elizabeth's sister is no better than she should be. Four: Frank, her own blue-eyed boy, is being unfairly threatened with dismissal by the factor. And I'm sure that wasn't the half of it.'

Nancy could tell by June's scarlet face that she was spot-on. 'As to the first allegation, you can make up your own mind!' she said. 'The next two are pure Isa poison. And the last one — well, I'm no admirer of Mr Shaw, but there's nothing unfair about it. Everyone knows Frank Robertson skives off work and stravaigs about the countryside breaking hearts. It's a wonder he's lasted this long in the job.'

June's mouth was hanging open. 'What does Frank do — he doesn't work on the farm?'

'He's the forester, like his father before him.' Nancy leaned forward and patted

June's hand. 'The best thing, dear, since you can't avoid Isa, is not to believe a word she says, and don't tell her anything about yourself.'

There was a clatter outside as a woman with windblown brown hair leant a bicycle against the wall. 'Oh, here's Peggy. I'll introduce you. She's a cousin of Elizabeth's. You'll soon get to know everybody!'

June put the stamps in her purse. 'I'm sure I will,' she said, looking rather dazed.

3

'Hello, darling.' Mamie knelt down and held out her arms, and Flora ran into them. Tibbie had tied Flora's hair in such tight little pigtails that they corkscrewed out rather comically behind her ears. Over her smocked dress she wore an olive-green cardigan, beautifully knitted in a complicated pattern. Mamie recognised the wool. Tibbie must have unravelled a jumper of her own to make it — it was a very grown-up colour for a wee girl.

Mamie stood up, lifting her granddaughter with her. 'Neil wanted to visit one of his cronies in the village, so I thought I'd come with him and catch up on the news from you all,' she said to Tibbie. 'Here, let me help.'

She sat down on the chair on the other side of the fireplace, with Flora on her knee, and reached for a sock to darn. The two grandmothers generally got on well.

17

With a smile, Tibbie handed her a ball of wool and a large needle. 'I'll need to knit Elizabeth another pair,' she said. 'This one's more darns than sock.'

'Where's Libby?' Mamie leaned to one side so that she didn't have the needle anywhere near Flora's face.

Tibbie's lips tightened. 'I sent her up to her bed for an hour. Answered me back, the little madam, when I asked her to finish her dinner.'

'Oh,' said Mamie in dismay. 'I'm sure she never meant to be rude.'

'It was a good plate of Irish stew. I've never known such a faddy child.' Tibbie's darning needle went in and out determinedly.

Mamie felt sure she wouldn't have been able to finish the stew either. Tibbie's knitting and sewing skills were second to none, but her cooking skills were not. No doubt the Irish stew would have had meat that was hard to chew and a layer of grease on top.

'Flora was a good girl, weren't you? You finished yours.' Tibbie smiled over at the

18

little girl, who squirmed and wriggled off Mamie's knee.

'Granny Mamie, look!' she said. 'Granny Tib's teaching me to sew.' She produced a square of cloth with a neat row of stitches across the top.

'You couldn't have a better teacher,' Mamie said.

Two years ago, Mamie had promised herself that, whatever the provocation, she wasn't going to interfere with the way Tibbie ran the household or her way of dealing with the girls. The last thing Elizabeth needed was her mother and her mother-in-law falling out. She hadn't broken that promise ... but she had bitten her tongue many a time to keep it.

Tibbie looked at the clock. 'You can tell Libby she can come down now, Flora. We'll say no more about it. You'll have a cup of tea, Mamie?'

As Flora scampered upstairs and Tibbie went through to the kitchen, Mamie heard the front door open and the telephone being lifted in the hall.

'It's Elizabeth Duncan. Is Andy

around? We've got a newborn calf; doesn't look too healthy … Andy? Can you come out? The mother won't let Tam or me near her. Wonderful — see you in half an hour.'

She popped her head round the sitting-room door and then came right in when she saw her mother. 'Mum, this is a nice surprise.' She came over and gave Mamie a quick hug. 'Sorry I can't stay. Just popped in to phone the vet — I was nearer the house than the office. Everything all right?'

'Your dad and I are fine.' Mamie lowered her voice. 'We've had a letter from Chris, but I don't want to talk about it in front of Tibbie. You know how disapproving she is of everything Chris does.'

'What's she been up to now?' Elizabeth didn't look worried, just amused, at the mention of her younger sister.

'I wish I knew. She sounded very mysterious. Here, read it when you have time.' Mamie took an envelope from her handbag and Elizabeth stuffed it into the pocket of her waterproof jacket.

'Don't worry, Mum. She's bound to live a completely different life down in London from us, up here in the wilds. I'll say hello to the girls and then I must dash. Oh, here they are.'

Libby rushed over to her mother. 'Mummy! Granny Tib says the poor children in Africa would be very pleased to have Irish stew to eat. Can we send it to them? I don't like it.'

Mamie bent over Flora to hide her smile. 'What's that you've got there, darling?' Flora was thrusting a rather damp bundle at her.

'I put it there when Granny Tib wasn't looking,' she whispered, and Mamie realised with a pang of horror that she'd just been given a handkerchief full of Flora's dinner.

4

Nancy was holding an airmail letter addressed to Alec Mackay, Peggy's husband. She turned it over. The sender was one Hugh Mackay, with an address in California. Must be a relative of Alec's, then. She seemed to remember something about a brother who'd left the area long ago, but getting any information out of Alec was like squeezing blood out of the proverbial stone. His face lit up and his toe tapped when he could be persuaded to play the fiddle, but otherwise he was as miserable as a month of wet Sundays. She didn't know how Peggy put up with him.

She went to the door and pulled down the 'Early Closing Day' sign. Her plans for the afternoon could wait. She'd take herself up to Glenmore and deliver the letter personally.

It was a winding two miles to get to the farm from the main road. It was shame

22

Peggy didn't drive, Nancy reflected. She was dependent on Alec for a lift if it was to somewhere she couldn't get to on her beloved bicycle. No doubt, though, the boys would be getting their licences soon. Colin must be seventeen on his next birthday, and Davy a year younger. Tests would surely be a formality — they'd been driving the tractor in their own fields for years. Why pay a tractorman when you had sons? But Alec would likely be giving the boys a wage now they'd left school. He wasn't a mean man, just a very thrifty one.

Peggy was washing the dishes from the midday meal. She dried her hands and took the airmail letter from Nancy. 'It's from America. California,' Nancy said.

'I see that. And I see that it's for Alec, so it'll have to wait until he comes in.' Peggy laid the letter on the dresser.

Nancy almost bounced with frustration. 'Do you know who this Hugh Mackay is?'

Peggy grinned at her old friend. 'Aye. That'll be Alec's nephew. But what he'll be writing to Alec for, I haven't a notion.'

'His brother's son?' Nancy wasn't going to give up.

'Yes, Jack's boy,' Peggy said. 'I say 'boy'; he'll be in his twenties now. Jack died a couple of years back — his widow wrote to tell us.'

'You never said.'

'There was nothing to say. Alec didn't want to talk about it. Jack was a few years older than him. He ran away after an argument with their father when Alec was a lad, apparently. That's all I know.'

'Well.' Nancy knew when to give up. She'd find out eventually anyway. She lifted the cat from the rug in front of the Rayburn, settled him comfortably on her knee, and prepared to talk of other matters. 'You'll be at the Rural on Wednesday?'

Peggy nodded. 'Do you think the lass I met in the post office the other day would be interested in joining?'

'I'll mention it next time I see her. Her man can surely look after the baby for a couple of hours. I feel for her, stuck

24

living next door to you-know-who, the wicked witch.'

'Her predecessor coped by not speaking to Isa at all,' Peggy remembered. 'But June seems to have a nice friendly manner about her, so I doubt she'll do that.'

'She's from down Glasgow way,' said Nancy knowledgably. 'Likes a bit of a laugh, I'd say, but she'll not get one with Isa.'

'We'll have to provide the laughs, then.' Peggy went to the cupboard and brought out a kitchen colander with bits of velvet and lace stuck onto it. 'This is my entry for the millinery competition on Wednesday. Looks like something the cat brought in, doesn't it?'

'I can only agree with you, dear,' Nancy chuckled. 'Mine looks much the same. And there's me, the Rural President! There's not much point in trying, though, is there? Tibbie will win as usual.'

Peggy stuffed the colander back where it came from. 'You're right. And we'll be the comic turn. As usual.'

5

It was half-past two. All Peggy's house-work and outside work were done, and she had a few hours before the evening chores. She hadn't seen Auntie Mamie for weeks. In the bad weather it would have been dangerous to cycle the three miles along the back road to the cottage Uncle Neil had fortuitously inherited from an elderly cousin the year before he retired.

After thirty-five years of living on a remote farm, gregarious Auntie Mamie had hoped that when they had to leave their tied house that they would rent one in Rosland village near other folk — including, of course, Elizabeth and her family. But she made the most of their new circumstances, transforming the hillside cottage from a bleak bachelor establishment into a warm and welcoming home that Peggy loved to visit. There was not much time or money in her own house for what Alec called 'frippery', and she didn't have Mamie's knack of making a place pretty on a shoestring.

Of course there were other tasks she could do this afternoon — start to prepare the spare room for the American visitors, for one thing — but the thought of getting her aunt's advice on the matter first propelled her outside and onto her bicycle.

She skidded to a halt outside the tractor shed. 'I'm off to see Auntie Mamie,' she called.

Alec came to the door. He tipped his cap back to scratch his greying curls. 'Mind yourself on that road,' he said. 'There might have been rockfalls after the snow.'

'I will,' she promised. 'Tell the boys there's fruitcake in the tin if they're hungry.'

★   ★   ★

Peggy had Mamie and Neil's full attention as she told them the contents of Hugh Mackay's letter. 'He says he's getting married in July to a wonderful girl called Donna, and they want to spend their honeymoon in Scotland. He's wondering if they could stay with us for a night or two — he'd love to see where his father grew up. It's a nice letter.'

'What did Alec say?'

'What does Alec ever say? Not much. But it affected him, I could see that. The boys had to ask who Hugh and Jack are. They're quite excited at the thought of having a cousin coming to stay. And, of course, California sounds just like the films.'

'I've heard about Jack but I've never met him,' Neil said. 'Did Alec tell the boys why he left?'

Peggy shook her head. 'Not really. Only that Jack and their father hadn't got on. I can't remember the last time we had visitors. I'll have to put heaters in that spare room; it feels damp. And the wallpaper's horrible, all faded and brown.'

'How about we redecorate?' her aunt suggested.

'Redecorate?'

'Yes.' Mamie jumped up. 'I've still got wallpaper samples from when I did our bedrooms here. I'd love to do your room if you want me to.'

'Do you mean it? Could you? It would make such a difference.'

'Mamie loves a new project,' Neil said as his wife left the room. 'I know she hoped to live in the village when I retired and get involved in all sorts of things, but it'd be daft to pay rent when we had this place handed to us. So thanks, Peggy.'

'Don't thank me — I'm very grateful to her. I'm slightly dreading the visit, I must confess. Hugh is kin to Alec, of course, but we've never met him and know next to nothing about him. He works in advertising, whatever that means.'

'Remember, the apple never falls far from the tree,' said Neil. 'Don't worry, lassie. I'm sure it'll all work out fine.'

Mamie put the samples on the table. 'There are some really bonny ones, Peg. Ten rolls will probably do that room. I'm going to the hairdresser in town tomorrow; I could pick them up then, if you like.'

Peggy opted for the paper with yellow roses and green leaves on a white background, as it was so light and fresh. But what would Alec say? Was new wallpaper a 'frippery'? She thought of the room as it might be seen through the eyes of a young modern couple. No, not a frippery. A necessity.

'How's all the family?' she asked. She'd talked about herself for long enough. 'Heard from Chris lately?'

Mamie and Neil exchanged a look. 'She does write regularly, I'll say that,' said Neil, tapping the ash from his pipe onto the hearth.

'She's moved into a new place, a flat with two other girls,' Mamie said. 'One designs dresses, and the other is a buyer in one of the big shops. She complains her own job is 'boring' compared to theirs.'

'The one in the bank?'

Mamie nodded. 'I'll have to quiz Robbie when he's home — you know, Robbie MacLean. He moved to London last month; he's with an accountancy firm. They see each other occasionally and he's a sensible boy. I hope he'll tell me what she's up to. Elizabeth doesn't think there's anything to worry about.'

'I'm sure she's right,' Peggy said, trying not to sound doubtful. You heard of such outlandish things going on in London.

Neil rose to look out of the window as a vehicle stopped outside the house. 'It's Alec.'

'Why is he here? I hope nothing's wrong with the boys.' Peggy went to meet him at the door.

'Thought I'd give you a lift home,' he said. 'That back road … '

'It was fine,' Peggy said, 'but thanks.' He was an old softie at heart! She linked her arm through his as they went through to the sitting room. 'Auntie Mamie says she'll paper the spare room for Hugh coming,' she said, aware that she was taking advantage of her aunt and uncle's presence to break the news. 'I've chosen this pattern. Isn't it pretty?'

Alec gave a noncommittal grunt.

'Don't be going to too much trouble. They'll have to take us as they find us.'

So that was settled. Peggy exulted inwardly. The guests' bedroom would look beautiful. The other rooms would look shabby in comparison, of course, but that couldn't be helped. And, she comforted herself, at least they'd eat well. She knew she could put on a good farmhouse spread. Her own produce too. They wouldn't have any complaints about that.

6

It was Flora's fourth birthday, but there was a present from their Auntie Chris for her sister as well.

Tibbie sniffed as the girls tore open the parcels and brought out organza dresses, Flora's cherry-red and Libby's kingfisher-blue, with net petticoats underneath. 'When in the world will they need to wear those?' she asked the assembled company.

Elizabeth picked Flora's dress up. It was a glorious colour and Flora would look adorable in it. It certainly wasn't practical, but trust Tibbie to look on the black side.

'Why don't you put them on now?' Elizabeth said. 'This is like a party, after all.'

It was such a shame Chris wasn't here to see them, she thought as the girls pirouetted around the room, fluffing the petticoats to make them stick out.

She hadn't been able to get home for Christmas either, because of the icy weather conditions, but had sent huge dolls for Libby and Flora that must have cost her most of her monthly wages.

Elizabeth stole a look at the photograph of Matthew, in pride of place on the mantelpiece and dusted lovingly by Tibbie every morning. What wouldn't she give for him to be here to see their little girls growing up, so different in personality although looking so similar. Both were fair-haired, like their parents, and both had Matthew's blue eyes rather than Elizabeth's grey ones. At almost six, Libby was dreamy and slightly timid, while Flora was outgoing and noisy. She didn't remember her father at all, and her older sister only did vaguely. It had broken Elizabeth's heart all over again when Libby came home after her first day at school last August and said, 'Everyone else in my class has got a daddy. Can we get a new one?'

'Time to blow out your candles, darling.' Mamie lifted Flora onto a chair and smoothed down the front of her dress so that it couldn't catch fire. Tibbie had provided the birthday tea — sausage rolls, thick cheese sandwiches and orange squash — but Mamie had made the big pink-iced Victoria sponge with sugar roses on the top.

Libby and Flora tucked into slices of cake, glistening in the middle with butter icing and raspberry jam. 'You'll be sick to your stomachs if you eat so fast,' Tibbie cautioned. 'We'll have to get the doctor to you.'

Elizabeth and her mother exchanged glances and looked away. 'Aren't the dresses ... ' said Elizabeth quickly.

'Have you heard ... ' began Mamie.

Elizabeth gestured for her mother to finish speaking.

'You'll have heard that they've appointed a locum doctor?' Mamie said, turning to include Tibbie in the conversation. 'Very young, from what I've heard. Quite a change from old Dr Munro.'

'He'll have new-fangled ideas, I don't doubt,' Tibbie said. 'Dr Scott — Struan

Scott, Nancy said he was called. Not long qualified from Aberdeen University.'

'He might be able to sort out your poor corns with some new-fangled method, Tib,' Neil said slyly. 'Dr Munro never managed to do that.'

Only Neil got away with teasing Tibbie. She gave a reluctant smile. 'I've been going to Dr Munro for years. He and Mrs Munro will be missed by many here.'

The girls stopped dancing around, ready to flop like puppies on the nearest adult. Flora cuddled up with her grandpa while Libby came and sat on Elizabeth's knee. Elizabeth held her close, savouring the moment — her two precious little girls, her parents and mother-in-law who did so much for her, a comfortable chair and a warm fire …

The doorbell rang.

Elizabeth groaned as she slid Libby to her feet and went to answer it. 'That'll be Tam. He was worried about one of the cows this morning, thought she might be having twins. Why couldn't she have waited until Monday? Give me some time with my own babies!'

It was Tam. 'I don't think we'll need the vet, Mrs Duncan. I've delivered twins before but I'll need some help,' he said grinning, as if he relished the prospect. He didn't seem to be cross about having to leave his fireside on a wet Sunday afternoon.

Elizabeth smiled back. 'Of course, Tam. I'll get changed. I'll be with you in about ten minutes.'

When she came back to the sitting room, Neil and Mamie were getting ready to go home, with the girls hanging on to them.

'Everyone's going!' Flora complained. 'What will we do now, Mummy?'

Elizabeth thought rapidly. Before Tibbie could tell the girls to stop their capers, she said: 'What about getting out your scrapbooks?'

Their Granny Mamie had made them each a scrapbook from wallpaper sample sheets cleverly sewn down one side. Tibbie heaved a sigh but she went to get newspaper to cover the table and the glue pot and scissors.

'When Granny Mamie was at the hairdresser's they gave her some old magazines to read, and she passed them on to me,' Elizabeth said. 'You can cut those up if you like. I'll bring them down.'

Upstairs, she changed quickly into her working clothes. The magazines were at the side of her bed, barely looked at because she was always asleep in two minutes — but she knew they portrayed a world so different from her own. A world of modern houses with brightly-coloured rooms and brand-new furniture. A world where women had wardrobes full of wonderful clothes, immaculate make-up and soft, manicured hands.

She found them fascinating but she didn't envy them. Her hands were about to help calves into the world — and the sight of a newborn calf, trying shakily to stand, was a thrill no matter how many times she'd seen it before.

She flicked through the magazines quickly in case there was anything

38

unsuitable for the girls to see — and stopped at one advertisement, her heart racing. She sat down on the bed to look at it properly.

No, she hadn't imagined it. The willowy figure in an elegant black dress, her blonde hair in a bouffant style, was her sister, Chris.

7

The twin calves had been christened Poppy and Pansy. As her long-legged offspring got their first feed of the day, their mother stood gazing benignly into the distance.

The names — bestowed on the calves by Libby and Flora — suited them, Elizabeth thought, leaning over the gate to admire the new arrivals. Poppy was mostly reddish brown, and Pansy had big white splashes.

Elizabeth and Chris had loved to name all the animals they grew up with: pet lambs, dogs, cats, and even — Elizabeth smiled to herself at the memory — a budgie called Vera Lynn.

Oh, what was she going to do about Chris? She hated the thought of keeping that picture a secret from Mum and Dad. Not that there was anything to be ashamed of. Chris looked lovely and the magazine was a well-established one, highly respectable, but as far as Mamie and Neil knew Chris worked in a bank. Oh well. It was up to herself to let their parents know about any changes in her life. Elizabeth didn't want to be the tale-telling big sister.

'Elizabeth!' The voice came from behind her and she turned to see Andy Kerr, the local vet. He'd been a couple of years above her at school, a quiet lad who'd maintained even as a small boy that he wanted to follow in his father's footsteps.

'Andy, hello. Nice to see you.'

'I was just passing — this is a social call,' Andy smiled. He inclined his head in the direction of the calves. 'These two are thriving. Tam and yourself did a good job there.'

'Your services were not required,' Elizabeth laughed. 'I'm going for my elevenses, Andy. You're welcome to share my flask and one of Tibbie's scones, if you've got time.'

'Thanks.' Andy accepted eagerly. 'I'd like to.'

'You haven't sampled Tibbie's baking before then?' teased Elizabeth. 'Luckily she's put lots of Mum's jam on it.'

She glanced at Andy as they walked over to the office. When she was little, up on the hill farm, she played a lot by herself because there were seven years between herself and Chris, so she was pleased when her shepherd father had to get the vet during school holidays because Andy usually came with him.

He always wanted to watch what his father did to administer to a sick beast but afterwards he could easily be persuaded to play hide and seek, or give Chris a piggy-back ride. At school he ignored her, of course — a big boy couldn't admit to playing with little girls!

When they moved up to the academy, they both caught the school bus. They never spoke, but he used to smile shyly at her. Their paths didn't cross again until long afterwards, when Elizabeth was married to Matthew and he got the farm manager's job at Rosland.

Fulfilling his childhood ambition, Andy

had taken over the vet's practice from his father.

Why had he never married, Elizabeth wondered now. He still had a shy smile which lit up his brown eyes. His stocky frame was strong enough to cope with farm animals, his hands gentle and delicate when they had to be. She knew from her dad that Andy had made improvements to the house he'd been brought up in, and where he now lived by himself.

All in all, he was probably the neighbourhood's most eligible bachelor.

'What? Have I got mud on my face?' Andy had caught her looking at him.

Elizabeth felt embarrassed, as if he'd heard her thoughts. 'No, but I have, on my hands. I'll go and wash them — you go ahead. You know where my cubbyhole is.'

Rodney Shaw, the estate factor, called to her as she passed his open door.

'I hope you're not forgetting that we have a meeting at twelve o'clock, Mrs Duncan?'

'Of course I ... '

He didn't let her finish. 'Why is Mr Kerr here? What's wrong? Is it the calves?'

'No, there's nothing wrong with the calves,' Elizabeth replied, through gritted teeth. She crossed her fingers behind her back. 'I wanted Andy's ... Mr Kerr's advice about something. Free advice,' she added. Not waiting for his response to that, she went to her own little office and shut the door behind her.

'That man!' she said as she poured Andy tea from the flask.

'You cope with him very well,' Andy said. 'It can't be easy, though.' He accepted half of a very large scone spread thickly with butter and rhubarb jam.

'He's always finding fault, trying to catch me out. I wish Lady Annabel would come up more often. He's so busy toadying up to her, I hardly see him.'

'Did I hear you saying to him you wanted my advice?'

'Er, yes. Well, I didn't think he'd appreciate you being here for a social call, even a brief one.'

Andy seemed to be enjoying Tibbie's

dry, hard scone. Elizabeth looked at him affectionately, remembering the boy she used to play with. She had an inspiration.

'Actually, I would like some advice,' she said, 'but not about the animals.'

She told him about the magazine picture of Chris modelling an expensive dress. It was a relief to tell someone, even although Andy turned out to be not much help.

'Modelling?' He shook his head. 'Don't know what your mum and dad will have to say about that, Elizabeth. But you're right. Chris should tell them about it herself.'

8

June carried an old travelling rug out to the front of the house and laid it on the grass. It was the last afternoon in May and for the first time since they'd arrived, she thought it was warm enough to sit with the baby outside. Not that Sadie could sit by herself yet, of course: she had to be propped up with a pillow and a couple of cushions.

June took her sewing bag out, and then fetched Sadie, looking adorable in her white sunbonnet and the latest matinee jacket June's mum had knitted. The haberdashers in Paisley were going to run out of pink wool at this rate!

They'd gone into town last Saturday, she and Tam and Sadie. It was much smaller than June's hometown, but the shops were a lot better than she'd somehow expected. Tam had bought her a pretty summery skirt she'd stopped to admire — she was worried they couldn't afford it, and thought any spare money should be spent on the baby, but Tam had insisted. It would have been nice if she'd been able to buy it for herself, though. Of course, she would rather be a mum than anything else in the world, but she did miss her wages from when she was a hairdresser.

Nancy, from their own village shop, had told her the best place in town to buy material and paper patterns. She'd picked out a colour from her new skirt to make herself a blouse with a round neck and three-quarter sleeves that had a ruffle over the elbow.

Although it wasn't finished, she'd taken the blouse along to show Nancy, who exclaimed over it and once again urged June to join the SWRI. The initials stood for 'Scottish Women's Rural Institute', apparently, and Nancy was the current President. They had competitions every month for things like baking and crafts and flower arranging. There was even a drama competition between the various institutes. June liked the idea of drama — she'd been in an amateur dramatic society back home — but wasn't sure if her domestic skills were up to the rest of it.

Plus, well, maybe she was being silly, but she'd never left Sadie before. It wasn't as if Rita would march in and demand her baby back — even if she did, Tam wouldn't meekly hand her over — and besides, the law was on their side ... but she didn't want to let Sadie out of her sight.

Although there was one good thing about the SWRI — June's next-door neighbour, Isa, didn't go, due to long-standing feuds with almost everyone in it. Isa had begun to tell June about them in detail one morning when they were hanging out their washing at the same time. June had listened without comment to the petty tales before she couldn't stand it any longer, and went indoors pretending she could hear Sadie crying.

She glanced at Isa's house now,

hoping that she wouldn't come out to join her if she saw her sitting on the lawn, a captive audience for more of her gossip.

Oh, no — Isa was waving. Before June could decide whether to respond or not, she realised that it wasn't herself Isa was looking at but her son, Frank, whose truck had drawn up.

Frank didn't wave back. He slammed the pick-up door shut and made to go to his own house, but stopped in his tracks when he saw June. With a brief glance at his mother standing behind their window he pushed open June's gate.

'Afternoon, Mrs Morrison.' He came over and squatted beside her, reaching out his hand to pinch the baby's cheek gently. 'Sadie, is that her name? A bonny girl — ' He glanced up at June. ' — just like her mum.'

Frank must take after his late father. With his height, fair skin and sunny ex-pression, he certainly looked nothing like small, pinch-faced Isa. And he was living up to his reputation, June thought with amusement. What was it Nancy had said about him? *He skives off and stravaigs around the countryside breaking hearts.* And even though he knew June's heart was elsewhere, he couldn't resist turning his charm on her.

'Have you finished work early today?' she asked innocently.

'Came home to get changed.' With a grimace Frank indicated the Rosland estate suit he wore — plus-four trousers and jacket in dark-green herringbone-patterned tweed. 'Bit of other business to attend to.' He winked at her as he stood up.

June couldn't help smiling back. It was easy to see why the girls in the area found him attractive, each one probably thinking that she'd be the one he'd settle down with.

'Frankie, are you coming in?' Isa was at their front door now.

'Just coming, Ma.' Frank fumbled in his jacket pocket and took out half-a-crown which he put into Sadie's little fist. 'A silver coin for good luck. See, she's

50

'holding on to it. That's a sign she'll be thrifty.'

'More than you are, giving your money away,' his mother sniffed.

Frank went red. 'Don't mind Ma,' he said in a low voice.

June had no intention of discussing Isa with her son. She took the half-crown before Sadie could put it in her mouth. 'Thank you. It's an old custom, isn't it, giving a baby a coin?'

Fifteen minutes later, she saw him leave the house wearing dark trousers and a fashionable striped shirt.

Isa came to the garden gate with him. 'What will I say if Mr Shaw wants to know where you are?'

'Say you haven't seen me since breakfast. He won't ask, though. I told him I'd be cutting out the weak trees from the far wood today.'

Isa leaned over June's gate when he'd gone. 'He's a hard worker, Frank is. Deserves a bit of fun.'

June didn't reply. She hoped that Mr Shaw wouldn't come looking for Frank and decide to ask her if she'd seen him.

As if she'd read June's mind, Isa narrowed her eyes. 'Frank's a hard worker,' she repeated. 'Don't you go making trouble for him.'

9

'I'll get it.' Mamie hurried into the hall to answer the phone. The noise of coins falling at the other end indicated the caller was in a phone box.

'Mum?'

'Chris! What's wrong?' She glanced at the grandfather clock. Half-past four. 'Are you at work?'

'No. Nothing's wrong — well, yes it is. We left London sometime in the middle of the night and we've been driving. We've had an accident — we're all right, don't worry. A deer ran out ... sorry, I've got hardly any pennies.'

'What? Where? Who's 'we'?' Mamie asked in bewilderment.

'Let me speak, Chris, you idiot.' A man's voice came on. 'Mrs MacPherson, it's Robbie McLean. We've gone into a ditch at the Lochend crossroads. Is there any chance ... '

Pip, pip, pip. Silence.

Mamie put the receiver down in frustration.

'Who was it?' Neil looked up from his newspaper. He laid it down on the table when he saw Mamie's face.

'Chris, and Robbie. They've driven up from London.' She held up her hands to stop her husband's exclamations. 'They're fine,' she said, 'but the car's gone off the road, at the crossroads. They need help to get it out.'

'I'll go up to Alec's, see if he can come with a tractor. Of all the hare-brained ...'

'I know, I know.' Mamie shook her head. 'Why didn't she let us know she was coming?'

As Neil was leaving, Mamie grabbed her coat. 'I'll come with you.'

'Don't worry. Nine lives, our Chris has, remember?'

Mamie thought of the times when Chris had got lost in the mist on the hill farm, when she'd climbed on the shed roof, when she'd almost fallen into the sheep dip — so many escapades.

'She did sound all right,' she admitted. 'But I want to see for myself.'

★   ★   ★

'Alec's coming with the tractor,' Neil told Chris and Robbie. 'You're taking him away from the potato field, so don't be surprised if he doesn't give you a great welcome.'

Chris looked contrite. 'We're really sorry. Robbie had to swerve to avoid the deer, otherwise it would have hit us.'

'That doesn't bear thinking about.' Mamie shuddered. She patted Robbie on the arm. 'I hope your car isn't badly damaged.'

'Thanks, Mrs MacPherson. Luckily I wasn't going fast. One of the lights is smashed. I can't tell if there's anything wrong with the engine until it's back on the road.'

Under his thatch of dark hair, Robbie's face was white. Mamie went to their own car and took out a packet of barley sugar.

55

'Here, Robbie' she said, 'sit down and have one of these. You've had quite a fright.'

Chris refused a sweetie. Mamie looked at her youngest daughter, perched on a gate and apparently none the worse for the experience, wearing a stylish pink-and-black frock and shoes with spiky heels. Her hair was in a French roll, her almond-shaped eyes were darkly outlined, and she wore pale, shimmery lipstick.

Neil must have been taking in his daughter's appearance too. 'Sheep kicked me in the face one clipping time, Chris. I had black eyes like yours for a week.'

'Ha-ha, very funny, Dad.'

Mamie smiled inwardly. Teenage Chris would have answered back rudely to her father's teasing but, at twenty-five, she'd learnt to keep her temper. Her rebellious days were over, thank goodness. And, Mamie couldn't help thinking, it would be lovely if Chris and Robbie were to be romantically involved instead of being just old school pals. It was time Chris settled down. Robbie was such a nice lad

— good-looking, too — and of course they knew his parents well, and …

'While we're waiting,' said Chris, 'I have something to say.'

Oh! Mamie flashed a smile at Neil. How amazing! Just what she'd been hoping for this very minute. An engagement!

'I don't want to be called Chris anymore.'

'What?' Mamie stared at her daughter, her heart plummeting with disappointment. 'You've always said you preferred Chris to Christine.'

'I do. But Chris sounds like a boy, and Christine's so old-fashioned. Sorry. I know you named me after Dad's mother, but this is 1963. From now on, I want to be called Crystal.'

'Crystal!' Neil expostulated. 'What kind of a name is that?'

'It suits me,' Chris — Crystal — said calmly, 'and it suits my new …'

'There's a tractor,' Robbie interrupted.

Alec tipped his cap in silent greeting as he got off the tractor and tied one end of a long rope to the back of it. He handed the other end to Neil to attach to the car bumper and climbed back into the driver's seat.

Neil raised his hand. 'That's it, Alec, pull away.'

He turned to get out of the ditch and suddenly put his hand to his back. A spasm of pain crossed his face.

'Oh no. Alec, stop!' Mamie called. 'Neil's back's gone.'

★ ★ ★

'Not the first time this has happened, I see from Dr Munro's records.' Dr Scott, the new locum, smiled ruefully at Neil. 'The remedy's same as before, I'm afraid. Complete bed rest.'

It had been a very long evening. Fortunately, Robbie's car was drivable — once they'd eventually got it out, and he drove Chris — *Crystal* — home. Mamie followed in their car, with Neil stretched out groaning on the back seat.

Once he was lying down on the sofa, Mamie had phoned the doctor while her daughter went to have a bath. Dr Scott said he'd come over as soon as he could, just as old Dr Munro would have done, which was a relief. Some folk in the area were grumbling about a few of the changes the young doctor had made but, in Mamie's private opinion, these were well overdue.

'Thank you for coming. I'll show you out,' she said, leading the way into the hall, just as Chris came downstairs.

She had changed into tight cotton trousers and a gingham blouse that tied at the waist. Her wet hair fell in waves around her face. She looked at the doctor, her eyes widening.

'Hello. I'm Crystal MacPherson.' She held out her hand.

He took it, staring back at her. It was as if they'd both forgotten Mamie was there.

'Struan Scott.' The doctor's voice was husky. He cleared his throat. 'Crystal. What a beautiful name.'

10

June held Sadie in her arms and looked out of the window.

'In just a wee minute, you'll see your daddy coming round that corner,' she said.

She laughed as Sadie grabbed a handful of her hair and tugged it. 'Ow! Look, there he is now.'

As she ran to the front door she glanced at the brown envelope on the kitchen table. It had taken every ounce of her self-control not to open it before Tam came home.

'It's here. It's arrived.'

Tam kicked off his wellies and dropped his jacket on the floor. His face paled under his ruddy complexion. He gave them both a quick kiss. 'Let's get it over with.'

A family adoption was a less formal process than the usual kind, but of course the authorities had to be assured that it would be in the baby's best interest. Tam's young cousin, Rita, was in no position to bring up a child by herself; and, knowing of Tam and June's longing for a baby, it had been Rita's own mother who had suggested that they adopt Sadie.

The new job at Rosland had come at a good time. Although they knew they would miss their families in the south-west of Scotland, Tam and June thought it best to put some distance between themselves and Rita. It had been a very difficult time for everyone involved.

Tam tore open the envelope. His eyes welled with tears.

'That's it,' he said. 'Sadie's ours.'

They had done everything properly and there had been no reason to suppose that there would be any hitch, but — June leaned against Tam feeling weak with relief — it was so wonderful to get confirmation in black and white.

As she hugged Sadie close, she thought of Rita, and hoped with all her heart that one day, in other circumstances, she would know the joy June was feeling now.

Tam put his arms round both of them. 'I want to tell the world!'

'The adoption is nobody else's business,' June said firmly. 'As far as everyone around here is concerned, she's our own flesh and blood.' That was half-true anyway. She handed Sadie to Tam. 'Would you like to give your daughter her bath while I make our supper?'

*   *   *

The outing to Dunrobin Castle was still to come, but this was the last meeting of the SWRI before the summer break.

Nancy handed over to her Vice-President.

'Peggy knows where to find me when she needs guidance,' she said with a twinkle in her eye as she stepped down to sit in the audience.

The new President smiled.

'Ladies, I'll try to fill Nancy's shoes. I hope ... ' Peggy broke off as the door opened.

In came June Morrison, from Rosland.

Good — Nancy had been encouraging her for a while to come along. A pity she'd left it till the last meeting, though. And behind her came — goodness, that must be Tam Morrison, holding a carrycot.

'Don't mind us,' Tam said cheerfully. 'Sadie and me will sit quietly at the back.'

Was there any reason why a man — or a baby, for that matter — couldn't be at a WRI meeting? Peggy wondered frantically.

Very red in the face, June tiptoed down the aisle to find a seat. Sympathy for her gave Peggy control of the situation.

'Come in, Mrs Morrison. You're very welcome. Now — ' She clapped her hands to regain the audience's attention. '— the first thing we have to do is allocate parts for the Federation drama competition in February. Remember, the play is called *For Love or Money*. Nancy wrote it and will produce it.'

Ten minutes later there was only one part left to be decided upon.

Nancy stood up. 'I wondered, June, if you'd like to take that on? You told me you belonged to an amateur dramatic society.'

June went scarlet again as everyone turned to look at her.

'Oh no, I'm sure there's someone else who … '

Forgetting his promise to be quiet, Tam Morrison called out, 'When the Paisley Players did *Little Women*, she was Jo, and everyone said she …'

'Tam! I … well, yes, I could — if no one else … ?'

'Good. That's settled,' Peggy said, as Nancy subsided, looking pleased with herself.

★   ★   ★

'Will you join us?' Peggy asked Tam when they broke for tea and cake.

'Thank you, Mrs … ?'

'Peggy Mackay,' said Peggy. 'I'm a cousin of Elizabeth Duncan's. You've likely met my husband Alec. He's visiting Elizabeth now while he waits for me. Will you be learning to drive, June? It would be nice to be independent of our menfolk, wouldn't it?'

For the third time that evening June looked embarrassed. 'I can drive,' she said, 'but … ' She seemed unwilling to continue.

'Well, I must refill that teapot,' Peggy said into the awkward pause.

Odd, she thought, as she waited in the kitchen for the water to boil. June seemed so friendly and outgoing, not the sort of woman afraid to do things on her own. But who was Peggy Mackay to give advice about driving? She made a face at her reflection in the kettle. Her heart thudded as it always did when she remembered the last time she was behind the wheel of a car. Would she ever be able to forget it?

11

'They've gone for a walk up the glen. Two days ago it was all the way to Inverness to the cinema — she wasn't back until after one. And ... '

'Mum,' Elizabeth interrupted gently, 'you don't need to lie awake listening for her coming home. She's a big girl now.'

'I know, I know.' Mamie laughed a little at herself. 'But it's all happened so quickly. She and Dr Scott — Struan — only met last week. She's told Robbie she's staying up for another few days and she'll get the train back. She's treated him disgracefully! Your father is more upset about that than about this modelling thing. He's sure that's just a phase — like wanting to change her name.'

After all her worrying about how Mamie and Neil were going to take the news about their younger daughter's new career, Elizabeth was surprised how calm they'd been.

Crystal — as Elizabeth was now trying to remember to call her sister — had told them that one of the girls she shared a flat with had introduced her to a photographer for the glossy magazine. Since that first job, Crystal had been taken on by a modelling agency, had had several other assignments, and given up her job in the bank.

Neil told her she was foolish to do that, abandon a steady wage coming in. He was left with his mouth hanging open in astonishment when she told him how much she'd been paid to look glamorous and wear a beautiful dress.

As for her name ... Mamie had suggested to Neil that they pronounce it in the same way but write it differently: Crys.

But treating Robbie as if he were her chauffeur was just plain rude in Neil's eyes. Although Robbie himself didn't seem to mind. Not that they'd seen much of him — he had his own family and friends to catch up with — but a few days after their dramatic arrival he'd appeared

67

with a coat belonging to Crys that had been left in his car.

He didn't seem surprised to hear of her change of plan; no doubt he was aware that she and the new doctor had been seen out together.

'That's them back now,' Elizabeth said, catching sight through the window of Crystal and Struan standing in the road. They shared a lingering kiss before Struan got into his car and drove away.

Crystal walked dreamily to the front door, stopping to replenish her lipstick before coming in.

'Elizabeth!' Obviously she had been too engrossed to notice Elizabeth's car parked at the side of the house. 'Are the girls with you?'

'It's Wednesday afternoon, Crys! Libby's at school.'

'Is it Wednesday already?' Crystal asked in amazement. 'I've lost track of time. That's what being in the country does to you.'

'That's what being out till all hours does to you,' her father put in, from his prone position on the sofa.

Crystal rolled her eyes at him. 'Can I come back with you for the night?' she asked her sister. 'I've hardly seen anything of my nieces.'

★   ★   ★

'So what's happening down on the farm?' Crystal asked as they made their way to Rosland.

'Oh, the usual. I dashed in to see how Dad was when I was up this way anyway. I had to see Alec. We've made a deal that he gets the use of one of our balers when the hay's ready — his own is beyond repair and he can't afford to replace it. In exchange, he'll send either Colin or Davie over to give us a hand with our harvest.'

'Sounds a good idea.'

'No doubt Mr Shaw won't agree with you.' Elizabeth sighed. 'He doesn't like these friendly arrangements.'

'Is Lady Annabel in residence yet?'

'Last time I asked Mr Shaw, he said she was due up next week. She'll be here off and on until September and the gillies' ball.'

'Oooh! You get invited to that, don't you? Could you wangle it that I do? Struan thinks he'll be here for another four months.'

'I'm not sure how I could do that, Crys. Anyway, I haven't been to it since … since Matthew.'

Crys put her hand on Elizabeth's arm. 'Of course. Sorry. But if you go this year, and I'm here, let me make you up and lend you a dress. You could be the belle of the ball with some expert help.'

Elizabeth laughed. No doubt Crystal was eyeing the unflattering dungarees she was wearing — a pair of Matthew's that Tibbie had altered to fit.

'I'll take you up on your offer in the very unlikely event I go. Look, there's Tibbie and Flora, and Libby's just come out.'

'Our old school,' Crystal said, nostalgically. 'It looks just the same.'

'I hope it will be the same for a long time. There are rumours it's going to close due to falling numbers.'

'They can't do that!'

The girls had seen Elizabeth's car and were waving frantically.

'Are you going to drive them home?'

Elizabeth shook her head. 'I'm meeting Mr Shaw at the top field in five minutes. He's got some scheme to have the hedge there pulled up. I'm hoping he'll change his mind.'

'You tell him, sis.' Crystal swung her long legs out of the car and ran across the road to where the little girls were jumping up and down in excitement.

Elizabeth blew them a kiss and then put her foot hard on the accelerator. She didn't want to give the factor any cause for complaint by arriving late.

The driver in an oncoming car held up his hand, motioning her to stop. He wound down his window. It was Andy Kerr.

'Where are you off to in such a hurry?'

'You know, doing my master's bidding.' Elizabeth smiled, keeping her engine running.

'I won't hold you up then,' Andy said. 'The Young Farmers' Club event at the show in August — I wondered if you were involved in that? I've been asked to give a demonstration.'

'I have said I'd help, yes.' Her hand hovered over the handbrake. 'Andy, can we talk about it another time?' She thought quickly. 'Come for a cup of tea on Sunday afternoon?'

His face lit up. 'See you then.'

★   ★   ★

The field gate was open. Mr Shaw must be there already, and … oh, no. There was another familiar vehicle there too — Lady Annabel's Land Rover, with the lady herself standing beside it.

'Lady Annabel,' Elizabeth stammered. 'I didn't expect you to be here.'

'Elizabeth, good to see you,' said Lady Annabel, shaking hands heartily. 'I came up last night. I wanted to be at an important county council meeting, and the date was brought forward to this evening.'

'I believe I did inform you that her Ladyship would be with us today, Mrs Duncan,' Rodney Shaw lied smoothly. He made a show of pulling back his sleeve and consulting his watch. 'Shall we get on? I think you've kept her waiting long enough.'

12

Elizabeth was still fuming over Rodney Shaw's duplicity the next morning when she went into the dairy.

'Is that the milk for the House?' she asked Tam. 'I'll take it up myself.'

'There you go, Mrs Duncan.' The dairyman handed her a pail. 'It's good creamy stuff! I hope her Ladyship enjoys it.'

'I'm sure she will. You're doing a grand job here, Tam.'

He flushed. 'Thanks, Mrs Duncan.'

'I was wondering — my youngest, Flora, is very keen on babies. She's been bothering my mother-in-law to take her to see your Sadie. Would it be convenient if they visited on Sunday afternoon?'

'June would love to show the baby off, I'm sure,' Tam replied, after a moment's hesitation. 'I'll tell her to expect them about three, shall I?'

'Good.' Elizabeth moved the heavy pail from one hand to the other. 'Right, I'll catch up with you later.'

It was really Tam's job to deliver the milk to the cook at Rosland House, but Elizabeth felt she had to find out if she'd gone down in her Ladyship's estimation after what happened yesterday.

The first sight that met her eyes as she drove up to the House was the rear view of Lady Annabel leaning into the engine of the Land Rover. She turned her head as Elizabeth carried on round to the kitchen door.

After the milk had been safely delivered, Elizabeth left her car and walked back to where Lady Annabel was wiping her fingers on an oily cloth.

'Learned how to strip an engine during the war,' she said, to Elizabeth's surprise. 'No point in paying someone else to do it.' She pulled the bonnet shut. 'Can you spare me half an hour, Elizabeth? Come in. I'll rustle up some coffee.'

Her Ladyship's attitude towards her was no different to any other time,

Elizabeth thought thankfully. But if Rodney Shaw was prepared to fib in front of Elizabeth to put her in the wrong yesterday, goodness knows what he'd been saying behind her back.

As she waited in the library while Lady Annabel went to wash her hands, Elizabeth looked at the huge gilt-framed portrait of the late Lord Mannering. They'd never seen much of him up here — he'd preferred to stay in the south, leaving Rosland in factor Rodney Shaw's hands. After his Lordship's death last year his elder daughter, Lady Annabel, had assumed the running of the estate here and the family's lands in England and Ireland.

It suddenly occurred to Elizabeth that Lady Annabel's evident affection for the Scottish estate, and her intention to be here for most of the summer, might not suit Mr Shaw. After doing things his way for so long, he now had a hands-on employer to answer to.

Lady Annabel looked like her father, Elizabeth mused, with her strong jaw and springy dark hair. Lord Mannering was probably in his early forties in the portrait, the same age as his daughter was now.

'Poor old Pop.'

Elizabeth turned to see Lady Annabel carrying a tray. She set it down and proceeded to pour Elizabeth a cup of coffee. It didn't feel right to be waited on by her employer — surely Lady Annabel would have taken on the usual number of local girls to staff the House for the summer?

'Sit down, Elizabeth. Milk?' Then, as if she'd been privy to Elizabeth's thoughts, Lady Annabel said, 'It won't make me popular, but I'm cutting back on indoor staff this year.' She glanced over at the portrait. 'Death duties. And then my stepmother … ' She stopped. 'Let's just say she has extravagant tastes.'

'Will we be seeing Lady Mannering at Rosland?' Elizabeth asked politely.

'Goodness, no. The South of France is much more to her taste,' Lady Annabel snorted. 'And to Cecily's, too — my young half-sister. You've got a younger sister, haven't you? I'm sure she doesn't give your parents any trouble?'

Elizabeth wondered how to reply, but as Lady Annabel seemed genuinely interested, she told her the latest news about Crys.

Her Ladyship listened carefully. 'I'm sure she won't get her head turned in London,' she said, 'with a family like yours behind her. I'm afraid Cecily's been dreadfully spoilt all her life. She's just twenty and her mother has no control of her whatsoever. I did wonder about getting her up to Rosland for a while; perhaps I can interest her in what, after all, is part of her inheritance, too. Maybe the gillies' ball in September would be an inducement.'

She put down her coffee cup. 'Now,' she went on, 'I'm afraid those aforementioned death duties mean cutting back on expenditure in all areas. Shaw has suggested some possible changes relating to the farm.'

She pushed a piece of paper across

the table. 'Let me know what's feasible. This is your area, Elizabeth. From now on you'll have a say in every discussion.'

Elizabeth sighed inwardly with relief — Lady Annabel was showing that she trusted her. But as she glanced quickly down the page relief turned to anger and dismay. Get rid of the dairy herd Matthew and she had so carefully built up? No! Whatever else happened, she couldn't allow that.

*   *   *

Elizabeth settled Libby at the table with a jigsaw and browsed the bookshelves for something light to read. Sunday afternoon. Feet up on the sofa. It was a time she looked forward to all week, a few hours to relax before the evening chores, and especially welcome today after the bombshell Lady Annabel had dropped.

And the house would be quiet without her boisterous youngest daughter around — she and Tibbie had gone to visit Tam and June, Flora sparkling with the hope that she would be allowed to push baby Sadie in her pram.

When the doorbell rang just as she was getting comfortable, Elizabeth looked over at Libby and put her finger to her lips. If they kept quiet, perhaps the caller would go away. But whoever it was persisted. She risked a glance out of the window and saw Andy Kerr's truck.

Oh no. She'd completely forgotten. She'd asked Andy to come round to discuss the Young Farmers' Club's involvement in the agricultural show.

She put on what she hoped was a welcoming smile and opened the door.

'You did say Sunday?' Andy's expression was crestfallen.

Obviously the smile hadn't been welcoming enough. She put her arm through his and pulled him through to the sitting room. 'It's lovely to see you, Andy. Sit down. I'll put the kettle on.'

When she came back from the kitchen he was crouching over the jigsaw searching for a piece of sky.

'Stay. I can't do it all by myself,' Libby

said, grabbing his jacket as he tried to stand up.

Andy laughed. 'Alright if I have my tea at the table, Elizabeth?'

Elizabeth put a cup beside him and the two heads bent over the puzzle again. It was a shame Andy didn't have a family of his own, Elizabeth thought. Libby was chatting away easily to him which was good to see — she was usually so shy.

'This is an excellent way to spend a Sunday afternoon!' Andy smiled up at Elizabeth, who found herself blushing, as if he'd read her mind. What was she thinking of? Andy was an old and valued friend, but why he didn't have a wife and children was none of her business.

13

Peggy surveyed the spare bedroom with a mixture of dread and hopefulness.

Alec had given the ceiling a quick whitewash, but — muttering that the American visitors should take them as they found them — would have nothing further to do with the redecorating project. Peggy persuaded their boys, Colin and Davy, to help her push the furniture into the middle of the room and cover it with dustsheets. Their reward had been to strip off the old wallpaper, a task they'd enjoyed amid much horseplay.

She'd taken down the heavy curtains to wash, although the thought of putting the horrible things back up even when clean was hardly to be borne. The carpet was horrible too, the colours that had once swirled over it faded to grey. Well, there was nothing to do except give it the sweeping of its life.

But Auntie Mamie had come over early this morning to put up the pretty white and yellow and green wallpaper, and she was going to stay overnight. Peggy hugged herself at the thought. Her own mother had died young and Peggy regarded her aunt as a beloved substitute. Spending time with her would be a real treat.

★   ★   ★

'There.' Mamie stood back when one wall was finished. 'Lovely choice of colours, Peggy dear.'

Peggy looked up from pasting. 'You are clever, the way you've matched the pattern. I do hope Donna likes it.'

'Why wouldn't she?' Mamie asked. She climbed up the ladder and waited for Peggy to hand her the pasted strip. 'The next bit will be tricky, round the window. Have you got curtains for it?'

'I washed them this morning,' Peggy said gloomily. 'You know, I think they're the blackout curtains put up in the war. We've not done a thing with this room since we got married — it's just the way Alec's mother had it.'

Mamie peered round the ladder, out of the window.

'It seems a shame to hide that view,' she said.

Peggy looked at the hill with its covering of heather, faint mauve now but with the promise of glorious purple to come.

'And it's not as if anyone can see in,' Mamie went on, 'except for the birds. You don't need heavy curtains. I've got some white voile at home. I'll run you up a pair with that if you like.'

'Are you sure?' Peggy reached up to squeeze her aunt's arm.

Mamie's gaze had fallen on the carpet. 'Why not get rid of that too?'

*　*　*

Late that night Peggy surveyed the room again, this time with joy.

The walls were papered and the evening sun streamed in the open window. The boys had been enlisted to lift the carpet and drag it downstairs. The brown-stained floorboards underneath were polished to a shiny finish and a braided rug, purloined from the landing, lay beside the bed. The bedroom was completely transformed from how it had looked this morning: fit for a queen, never mind American relatives.

'It's beautiful, just beautiful, Auntie Mamie.' Peggy pushed a straggly lock behind her ear. 'Would you like a wash? I've put out a towel for you.'

Alec came into the room in his stocking feet. 'Let's see what you've been up to.'

'Do you like it?' Peggy asked eagerly.

'Hope the Yanks appreciate it,' Alec grunted. He nodded at Mamie. 'How's that man of yours?'

Mamie shook her head. 'Driving me mad,' she said. 'He makes a very bad patient. He's on his feet now, or I wouldn't have left him on his own — Crys has torn herself away from Dr Scott and is back in London at the moment — so he's desperate to get into the garden.

I said I'd much rather buy vegetables rather than have him laid low again.'

Alec gave a bark of laughter. 'I could spare Davy for a few hours on Sunday if you like.'

'That would keep us both happy. Thank you, Alec, we'll look forward to seeing Davy. Now, I must have that wash.'

Auntie Mamie still looks tidy despite her hard work, thought Peggy, catching sight of herself in the dressing-table mirror. What a fright her hair was! She hoped Alec would have time to drive her into town to get it tidied up before the visitors came. Of course Mamie would take her, or Elizabeth, but why should her relatives have to chauffer her about? It was too much to ask of them.

14

Davy looked like both his mum and his dad, Mamie thought. He had Peggy's hazel eyes and his hair was sandy-fair like Alec's, although his was greying now. But, unlike Alec, Davy was a cheerful lad, uncomplaining about being sent over to help his great-aunt and -uncle, Mamie and Neil, with their garden.

His mum, Peggy, would have liked him to stay on at school — his teachers had tried to encourage him too. But it made no sense, Alec said, to employ someone outside the family when he had his two boys to work with him on the farm. Mamie wondered what Davy would have done if he'd been given the choice.

This afternoon he'd made drills in the soil and sowed the carrot seeds. He'd planted out the leeks, mown the grass, and now he and Mamie were engaged in the never-ending task of weeding while

Neil sat, unwillingly idle, and smoked his pipe.

'Are you looking forward to meeting your cousin?' Mamie asked Davy as they knelt side by side at the flower-bed.

'Aye. We never even knew Dad had a brother who died in America. Jack. Why did he go to America, me and Colin were wondering?'

'I'm afraid I don't really know, Davy. I think there was a family quarrel years and years ago. But it's nice that Jack's son wants to see his Scottish family.'

'S'pose he wants the farm?'

'What do you mean?' Mamie sat back on her heels and looked at him.

'Well, see, me and Colin were thinking. Uncle Jack was older than Dad, so the farm would have been his by rights if he'd stayed. Farms always go to the oldest. So maybe this cousin should have it.'

'I don't think he could even if he wanted it, not after all this time,' Mamie said gently. Maybe Davy was also thinking that, as Alec's youngest son, he himself wouldn't be inheriting the farm.

She glanced over at Neil and raised her eyebrows. Neil rose to the occasion.

'I don't think he'd have a claim on it at all, Davy,' he said. 'Besides, what does he know about farming?'

'Dunno. In his letter he said he was in the advertising business. I asked Dad what that was but he didn't know.'

'I'm not sure either,' Neil confessed. 'But I bet our Crys would be able to tell you.'

'She'll be home again soon — or I can ask her when she phones. Don't worry about the farm, Davy,' Mamie said.

'I'm not.' Davy rubbed a grubby hand over his face. 'Anyway, Dad says small farms are just a way of losing money. I don't s'pose cousin Hugh will want to lose money.'

'Always looks on the bright side, your dad, eh?' Neil grinned.

'Hey, Uncle Neil,' Davy grinned back, 'd'you think Hugh will wear one of those big cowboy hats like in the films?'

'I wouldn't be surprised.' Neil winked at him.

'That would be a sight for sore eyes around here!' Mamie turned back to the weeds. 'Well, we'll find out soon enough.'

15

June hurried past Mrs Duncan's house on her way up to the main road, not wanting to attract the attention of Tibbie or Flora after the awkward visit last Sunday afternoon.

Of course she wanted to be friendly — this was Tam's boss's family, and she'd been shown nothing but kindness by them — and she'd gone to a lot of trouble to provide a nice afternoon tea. But she'd been apprehensive when Tam had said that little Flora wanted to see the baby, and sure enough, Flora seemed to think that Sadie was to be played with as if she were a doll and not a living being.

She'd sat down and spread her summer dress to make a lap, then held out her arms, evidently expecting June to just hand Sadie over. June had muttered something about the sugar bowl and retreated to the kitchen, Sadie on her hip.

When she came back, Tam was trying to interest Flora in their newly-acquired kitten, but Flora would have none of it. She made a beeline for Sadie, patting her hand and waving her rattle at her. It was sweet, and June wished she could relax, but instead she busied herself with pouring milk into cups and passing plates, clutching Sadie to her all the while.

Eventually, after they finished tea, she'd had to give in and put Sadie on Flora's knee, keeping a very tight hold of her. When Flora asked for the third time if she could take Sadie for a walk in her pram, Tibbie intervened and told her it was time for them to go home.

When they'd gone, Tam had been un-characteristically tight-lipped; but after Sadie was in bed, he'd put his arm round June and said carefully, as if treading on eggshells: 'Junie, Sadie is ours. No one's going to take her away. You could have been nicer to the wee girl.'

As she walked along to the village post-office-cum-shop, June thought of how difficult it was to put her feelings into words. It wasn't because the baby was adopted that she couldn't bear to let her out of her sight, and that she didn't like anyone other than herself or Tam to hold her. She would feel this way if she'd given birth to Sadie, she was sure. Her arms felt empty when the baby wasn't in them, and she worried when she couldn't see her, even when she was just upstairs, tucked into her cot. She looked at Sadie now — safe and asleep in the pram, but so small and helpless and precious — and yearned to pick her up.

Of course, as Flora was only four years old, even Tam wouldn't have let her take Sadie out on her own. But sometime, he said, maybe they could all go for a walk and let Flora push the pram? June had nodded agreement, though intending to put off that moment for as long as possible.

And then there was their next-door neighbour, Isa. She'd actually offered to look after Sadie any time June wanted! As if a mother wouldn't want to look after her own baby all the time.

Through the shop window she could see that several people were waiting to be served. No room for the pram. From behind the counter, Nancy caught her eye and waved. She waved back, and kept walking.

On the other side of the road was the school that Sadie would go to when she was five — although there was a rumour that the council wanted to close it, in which case she'd have to go all the way into town, which was a horrible thought.

It must be break-time because the children were out in the playground. Some were playing hopscotch and some were kicking a ball. Others were involved in some running-around game, bumping into each other and making a lot of noise. June shuddered to think of her little girl in the middle of them.

Next door to the school was the church. The minister had paid them a visit and had seemed very nice. Maybe they should think about getting Sadie christened there.

She passed the hall which she'd been

in for the WRI meeting. They'd been a friendly crowd who made her welcome. If they thought it odd that she was there with her husband and her baby, they didn't say so to her face. Well, they'd be seeing a lot more of Tam and Sadie once rehearsals started for the drama competition!

The only building to be seen now was the Rosland Inn, down a driveway and half-hidden by trees, before the pavement came to an end. She turned and retraced her steps.

The shop was still busy. And Sadie was still asleep, her tiny fist tucked under her chin. June had to go into the shop — there were several grocery items she needed, and she had her Family Allowance to collect.

Well, there was only one thing for it.

She put the brake on the pram and gently lifted Sadie up. The baby made no reaction to the move until June stepped through the door and set the bell jangling, upon which she opened startled eyes and howled.

June shushed her, rocking her back and forth. Then, before she knew what was happening, one of the customers — a lady she recognised from the WRI night — scooped Sadie from her.

'I'll mind the bairn, Mrs Morrison. You get on with your shopping.' She laid Sadie over her shoulder in a capable manner and patted her on the back.

June opened her mouth to protest, but the other customers were kindly urging her forward. Unwilling to make a fuss, she went to the front of the queue. She asked Nancy for what she wanted, feeling her voice shake. As she moved to the post office part of the shop, she saw that Sadie had calmed down and was engaged in chewing on the lady's scarf.

Nancy handed over the Family Allowance. 'Babies are a worry, aren't they?' Before June could make some noncommittal remark in reply, Nancy went on cheerily, 'Wait until you've got half a dozen. You'll be too busy to worry about them!'

June smiled back through gritted

teeth. Of course, Nancy couldn't know that Sadie was going to be June's one and only. But what could she, with no children of her own, know about worry?

16

Alec had done his own kind of redecorating in anticipation of the visitors, Peggy observed, as she washed the breakfast dishes — although he would never admit it. The tools and pieces of machinery that usually littered the farmyard had been tidied against the barn wall, and the yard had actually been swept.

The weather was doing its bit too. Today's glorious sunshine was due to last for the rest of the week.

Alec and the boys had just left the house to spend the day stacking hay in the field by the road. It would be the perfect sight to greet Hugh and Donna this afternoon — their postcard from London had said that they would get the train to Glasgow where they would hire a car and arrive at the farm about three o' clock.

The pantry was well-stocked. For tonight's meal there would be eggs from their own hens, lettuce from the garden. She'd cooked a big ham and made — the pièce de resistance — a delicious-sounding rhubarb tart, with orange rind in the pastry, from a recipe in this week's *Scottish Farmer.*

She would put the living-room to rights and make pancakes to eat, nice and fresh, with a welcoming cup of tea. And she'd spend a bit of time on her appearance — get changed into her best frock, put on powder and lipstick, and try to do something with her hair.

The back door banged open. Alec stormed into the kitchen and grabbed the car keys from their hook.

'What's happening? Where are you going?' Peggy dried her hands and stared at him.

'Fool of a boy, Colin. Left the ignition on overnight. Tractor won't start. I'll have to go into town for a part.'

Peggy looked at the clock and made a quick calculation. They'd be in town at nine — maybe the hairdresser could see her. There would be no time for a trim but perhaps her hair could be pinned up neatly with some of that spray stuff to keep it in place.

She tore off the pinny she wore in the mornings and smoothed down her old summer dress. No time to change. 'I'll come with you.'

In the car, as they arrived in town, she risked a glance at Alec. His expression was still thunderous.

If we had a phone, you could have called someone from the garage to come up, Peggy thought. But that was an old argument to be rehashed another day.

'Are the boys carrying on with it by themselves, with the hay?' she asked.

'Yup, not going to waste this weather. Where did you say you wanted to go?'

'Castle Street. Hairdressers. Shall I come to the garage after?' Peggy reached for the handle.

Alec nodded. 'Don't be more than twenty minutes. Wait.' He held out his arm to stop her closing the door. 'Peg. You're not getting it cut, are you?'

''Course not, you old silly.' Peggy was

smiling as she walked off. Alec had loved her long hair since their courting days. Twenty years on, she would really like to get it cut and permed. But as long as Alec remembered her as the girl she'd once been, she knew she never would.

She looked at herself in the mirror fifteen minutes later and saw that the hairdresser had done a grand job in the time. As she came out of the salon a car came to a sudden stop beside her and the driver leaned across and wound down the window.

'Peggy, you're in town early this morning.' It was Elizabeth.

'Alec had to come in to the garage.' Peggy patted her hair. 'I took the chance to get a 'do'.

'Are you meeting him there? That's where I'm going. Hop in.'

Peggy climbed gratefully into the passenger seat. Now she wouldn't be late.

'Is it today Alec's nephew's coming?' Elizabeth asked.

'They're due about three,' Peggy said, admiring the confident way Elizabeth drove, one hand on the wheel. 'I'm kind of nervous about it. I've never met any Americans before.'

'I'm sure they won't be much different from ourselves,' Elizabeth laughed. 'And Hugh's half a Mackay, after all.'

'Well, maybe it will be all right. They're here until the weekend. Will you be able to come up? Give me moral support. Bring the girls.'

'I'll try. Saturday, probably,' promised Elizabeth. 'And there's something I want to talk over with Alec. Rodney Shaw stuff.'

'Is he still making life difficult for you?'

Elizabeth stopped in the garage forecourt. 'Not half. But I'm used to him. Here we are, Peggy, and there's Alec, in a hurry to get off by the look of him.'

* * *

'What the … ' Alec thumped the steering wheel. 'Where are they?'

Peggy saw the hay waiting to be made into rucks and the half-finished stack,

102

but of the boys who were supposed to be working in the field there was no sign at all.

'Look!' she clutched Alec's arm, as they approached the house. 'There's a car. It must be them.' Her voice rose. 'Hugh and Donna. They're here!'

'Oh, for Pete's sake,' Alec grumbled. 'We'll never get the hay finished at this rate.'

But Peggy's hand had flown to the pull down the mirror on the sun-shade. For a change, she didn't have a hair out of place but the updo's elegant stiffness sat oddly above her ancient cotton dress and rather shiny face.

The bedroom was perfection, of course, she comforted herself, but she hadn't tidied and dusted the living-room, or washed the best china. Or made the pancakes. And the plans she'd had for the midday picnic in the hayfield would have to be abandoned, and a proper meal served.

'Peggy, are you getting out of the car or not?'

'Sorry.' She tried to pull herself together. As she headed for the back door she was aware that Alec hadn't followed her — off to lurk in the barn probably, to postpone the moment of meeting his unknown relative.

The first thing that registered with her as she went through the kitchen door was that the rhubarb tart was on the dresser, cut into crumbly slices. The second thing was Davy, lying back in Alec's chair with one leg up on a stool. And the third was Marilyn Monroe sitting at the kitchen table.

Peggy's head was in a whirl, but her hospitable instincts took over.

'My dear, you must be Donna,' she said. The blonde vision in front of her looked as much out of place in the farm kitchen as if she really were the famous film star. 'It's wonderful to see you.'

'It's wunnerful to be here.' Donna smiled, showing very white teeth. 'I think your house is so quaint.'

'And Hugh?'

'He wanted to have a look round,' Davy

said. 'Col's with him.'

Peggy turned her attention to her son. 'Why on earth are you sitting like that, Davy?' Now she came to look at him more closely she could see he was rather pale. 'Are you all right?'

'I fell off the stack and dunted my ankle.'

'What?'

'The boys were so sweet, Auntie Peggy,' Donna put in. 'Colin cut us some of this pie.' She indicated the untouched pudding in front of her.

'Right, I see.' Peggy rubbed her forehead. The ruin of the lovely tart was the least of her worries. She tried to think what to do first.

'I'll get your dad in to look at your ankle,' she said to Davy.

'Hugh said he'd drive me to the emergency room,' Davy said importantly. 'That's what they call the casualty department, in America.'

'I hope it won't come to that. Donna, would you like a cup of tea?'

Donna shook her head. 'Could I have

a glass of iced water?'

Peggy ran the kitchen tap for a minute before filling the glass. It didn't exactly feel icy to the touch but it was nice and cold.

'There you go, my dear. Now, excuse me, I'm just going to find Alec.'

She went out into the yard and saw Colin with a tall man of about thirty. For a moment she wondered if she'd somehow gone back in time. It was Alec as she remembered him from years back. A full head of sandy-fair hair above a high forehead, his face unlined, speedwell-blue eyes shining with enthusiasm.

Then the man who looked like Alec saw her and the spell was broken — he too had a gleaming Californian smile.

'Auntie Peggy? I'm Hugh Mackay.'

Before Peggy could respond Alec came, almost at a run, across the yard. To her astonishment she saw that his eyes were full of tears.

'Jack's lad!' He enveloped Hugh in a bear hug. 'You've come home.'

17

True to her word, Elizabeth took Libby and Flora up to Glenmore Farm early on the Saturday morning after the American guests arrived.

By that time she was frankly curious to meet them. Stories about Hugh's uncanny resemblance to his Scottish family, and his wife's glamorous appearance, had made their way to Rosland.

Peggy came across the farmyard to greet them.

'Donna's having a bath,' she whispered as Elizabeth got out of the car. 'She couldn't believe we didn't have a shower like she does at home.'

Elizabeth held the back door open for the girls. 'I hear she's very pretty,' she said in a normal tone.

Peggy glanced up at the bathroom window. 'She takes hours to get ready,' she said, her voice still low. 'Not that she wants to go anywhere.'

'And what's Hugh like?'

Peggy's face softened. 'He's so nice, and appreciative of everything. He's thrilled to be here.' She put a slight emphasis on the word 'He's'.

'That's understandable,' Elizabeth said, feeling rather sorry for Donna. After all, this was her honeymoon trip. 'He'll have heard about the place from his father.'

'It's some tale I can tell you, about his father — Jack — leaving here after an argument.' Peggy was whispering again. 'I know all about it now. I'd gathered before that Alec's father was a harsh man but I never thought ... Apparently, when Jack wrote home years later and said he was married with a little boy their father wouldn't ... Oh, there's Hugh. I'll tell you later.' She beckoned over the man who had just emerged from the house. He was wearing a pair of old blue dungarees and his shirtsleeves were rolled up.

'Hugh, this is my cousin, Elizabeth, and her daughters, Libby and Flora.'

'Good to meet you, Elizabeth' Hugh said. He had freckly forearms, just like Alec and Colin and Davy. 'Alec was telling me about you, running the big farm. I'd sure like to come see it.' As he spoke he bent down to smile at the girls. 'So y'all must be kind of cousins to me too. I've got a big clan of relations I never knew about!'

Elizabeth warmed to him immediately. 'How do you like Glenmore?'

'It's ... ' Hugh began, straightening up. 'It's not easy to put into words what it means to me to be here. You know, my dad could remember every stick and stone of the place. I felt at home the minute we arrived — and what a great welcome we got from these folks here.'

Peggy smiled, rather fixedly, Elizabeth thought. 'Hugh and Donna arrived before Alec and I got back from town ... '

'I couldn't wait to get up here,' Hugh interjected. 'Once we'd got to Glasgow I wanted to keep heading north.'

' ... so they were left to the tender mercies of the boys for an hour or so.'

'How is Davy?' Elizabeth asked. The stories the postman had brought down from Glenmore to Rosland had included Davy's accident.

'He won't be able to put his weight on his ankle for a while,' Peggy sighed. 'So we're a man down for the hay-making — well, I shouldn't say that, because Hugh's been pitching in as if he'd done it all his life.'

'Glad to help. And it gives Uncle Alec and Colin and I a chance to get to know each other. Uncle Alec sure has some good stories of when he and Dad were boys.' Hugh grinned. 'I'll be off back to the field, Auntie Peggy. See y'all later.'

'I don't remember Alec ever being so talkative,' Peggy said, as Hugh strode off. 'He never told our lads about any of these escapades he's coming out with now. Poor Davy. He doesn't care about missing the hay, but he hates being stuck inside with me and Donna. Maybe you three can cheer him up.'

Libby and Flora needed no second invitation. 'Is Tomcat there?' Libby asked.

Unfortunately, their granny was allergic to fur so they couldn't have a cat at home.

Peggy nodded. 'Davy is supposed to be unravelling binder twine — Alec doesn't like seeing him idle. Tomcat's not exactly helping.'

Inside, Davy was lying back with his bandaged ankle up on a stool, dangling pieces of the thick hairy string that was used to tie up hay bales. Tomcat watched, his paw poised ready to strike.

Davy sat up straight when he saw Peggy and began taking out knots. 'This is really hard,' he grumbled, as the girls ran to take over playing with the cat.

'That'll teach you to go jumping off hayricks,' his mother told him. 'If Hugh hadn't been here, your father would have been in a right fix.'

And *she* was in a fix too, Elizabeth realised. The arrangement she'd made with Alec — that in exchange for a loan of the estate baler, one of his boys would give a couple of days' labour at Rosland farm — might not be possible now if Davy wasn't recovered by harvest time.

Rodney Shaw would have plenty to say about that.

Peggy spooned instant coffee into cups. Overhead there was the sound of water draining out of the bath.

'I'd love to see the room you and Mum decorated,' Elizabeth said.

'I didn't do much,' her cousin said. 'Auntie Mamie did the papering and made lovely curtains and everything. *She* — ' Peggy jabbed a teaspoon in the direction of the ceiling, '*She's* got *wall-to-wall cream carpet* in her bedroom at home, apparently. And *pale peach* walls. Not '*that old-fashioned paper*'.'

'She doesn't live on a farm,' Elizabeth said gently, seeing that Peggy's delight in the room had been spoilt. 'Nor does she have children. Cream carpet — can you imagine!'

Peggy smiled reluctantly as she handed Elizabeth her coffee.

'She doesn't want to do anything,' she said, sitting down at the table. 'Of course, with me not driving it's difficult, but when I've suggested walks, cycling, getting the bus to town — she's got no interest in seeing anything.'

'She doesn't like shortbread,' Davy put in. 'In America, cookies — that's what they call biscuits — are the size of saucers, she said.'

'How long are they staying? I could come and get them, show them around the estate,' Elizabeth offered. It sounded like Peggy needed a rest from her visitors, the female one at least. 'Maybe Rosland House will impress her.'

'That would be good of you,' Peggy said gratefully. 'They were to stay for four days but we could see Hugh wanted to stay longer. I know it must be strange for Donna here — it's not her family history and she's a real city girl. She looks like a film star, doesn't she, Davy?'

Davy put down a piece of string. 'Her nails are out to here,' he said, indicating an unlikely inch from the end of his own stubby fingers. 'And they're red.'

'Goodness,' Elizabeth laughed, contemplating both her own and Peggy's short, unadorned nails. She put down her cup. 'Peg, do you mind if I go and have a word with Alec?'

Peggy jumped up. 'You can take their piece with you.' She indicated a basket with three mugs and a paper bag of scones. 'I'll fill the flask.'

★ ★ ★

The men hailed her gratefully and came to sit at the edge of the field to have their mid-morning cup of tea.

As Hugh regaled Colin with the delights of California — soda fountains, drive-in movies, Death Valley, ranches the size of Sutherland — Elizabeth told Alec about Rodney Shaw's proposal to do away with the dairy herd at Rosland.

'He's taking revenge, isn't he?' Alec said wrathfully.

Elizabeth nodded, unable to speak for the lump in her throat.

Three years earlier, Rodney Shaw had wanted to buy expensive new cowsheds. Elizabeth's husband, Matthew, had gone over the factor's head and told Lord

Mannering bluntly that his money would be better spent on buying more cows, improving the herd. His Lordship had agreed.

Now it was payback time.

18

'I hate sitting still!'

Mamie had to laugh. Not only was her husband Neil, having his movements restricted for fear of putting his back out again but now their great-nephew Davy was confined, for the moment, to a deck-chair in her garden.

When Mamie had gone over to Glenmore to meet the American visitors, Peggy had complained about Davy getting under her feet in the kitchen so she'd volunteered to take him back with her for a couple of nights. She could hardly do the same with Donna who seemed equally to be in Peggy's way.

Davy hulled a strawberry and dropped it into the bowl by his side. 'Col's having all the fun,' he moaned. 'I wanna hear about California, and show Hugh how to milk the cow.'

Mamie suppressed a smile at the sound

of the twang in Davy's voice. 'I couldn't believe how much Hugh looks like you all,' she said. 'He's a Mackay all right.'

'Crys says that advertising is telling folk about what you've made,' Neil said. 'It's big business, it seems. He'll be doing well, your cousin Hugh.'

'He showed us a picture of their house. It's about three times the size of ours.' Davy held his arms open wide. 'And his car was outside the house. It was huge as well. Everything in America's huge, seems to me.'

'They have more space,' said Neil. 'So, Davy-boy, did you find out what the quarrel was about? The one that sent Jack across the Atlantic?'

'Uh-huh.' Davy took a bite out of a particularly large strawberry, dribbling juice down his front. 'I can't get upstairs 'cause of my ankle so Mum made a bed for me in the wee room off the kitchen. And the first night, after everyone else went to bed, Dad and Hugh sat up talking. I think they forgot I could hear. But I could, every word.'

Mamie frowned at Neil. 'You shouldn't tell us, Davy, if it's private.'

'Mum told me and Col bits of it anyway the next day, and she told Elizabeth on Saturday.' Davy handed Mamie the bowl. 'That's the strawberries done.' He leaned back in the deckchair. 'First, Dad asked Hugh if he knew the old story. And Hugh said he didn't. His father, Uncle Jack, told him all about Alec and the farm but he'd never talked about why he left.'

Davy paused. A bee buzzing around the roses was the only sound to be heard.

'Dad said, well, one day the barn burnt down and their father, his and Uncle Jack's, said Jack must have been smoking in it. He wouldn't believe Jack when he said he hadn't. And the next morning when their father called upstairs for Jack to get his lazy hide out of bed he wasn't there. He'd left in the middle of the night.'

'Good grief.' Neil put down his pipe and stared at Davy.

"Your lazy hide', that's what he shouted upstairs,' Davy repeated with relish. 'Someone said later they'd seen

Jack getting on a train in Inverness. And it wasn't him smoking. Someone else's barn caught fire the next day and they caught a tramp running away from it.

'And guess what, Uncle Neil?' Davy went on. 'Dad said he was sorry for everything and the farm was Hugh's by rights. But Hugh said, no, there's nothing for you to apologise for. It worked out well for my dad. There are a million opportunities in California. He had a good life.'

'Well, that's some story,' said Neil. 'But your Uncle Jack surely died young? He was just two or three years older than Alec and he's, what, just past fifty?'

'Is he? I dunno,' Davy said. 'Uncle Jack fell off the roof of a house he was building. Jings!' He sat up, better to see the vehicle that had stopped at the garden gate. 'Who's that?'

The driver tooted the horn and waved.

'Crys said she'd bought a car,' Mamie said to Davy. She shook her head. 'Just look at it.'

Neil began to laugh. 'One of those

Minis. What colour would you say it was, Davy?'

'It's pink!' Davy said, evidently struggling between being disgusted and impressed. 'It's like this mark on my shirt. Strawberry pink.'

19

It was still warm and sunny at eight o' clock as Peggy saw Elizabeth's car draw up at Glenmore the following Wednesday.

Hugh had not wanted to leave his uncle in the lurch and had insisted on working in the field every day, so the visit to Rosland had been arranged for an evening.

Much as she would have liked some time at home without Donna being around, Peggy asked Elizabeth if she could come with them, and be dropped off at June Morrison's house. She had June's copy of the script for the WRI drama competition to give her.

'I could put it in the post,' Peggy explained to Elizabeth, 'but I want to check that she doesn't regret agreeing to be in the play. It is quite a commitment.'

Donna had changed out of the dress and high-heeled shoes she'd been wearing and put on blue slacks and a white blouse. The red of the cardigan slung round her shoulders exactly matched her sandals. She still looked dazzling, made up to the nines, but at least was dressed in more reasonable attire for looking around a working farm.

'You sit in the front, Donna,' Peggy said, nipping in behind Elizabeth. 'There's a lovely view from the top of the glen.' She didn't like the thought of Donna sitting with Hugh, whispering about how bored she was going to be, but she felt rather guilty when she saw how cramped it was in the back for Hugh's long legs.

To her surprise though, when the view spread before them, the low sun glowing over the purple hillside and the river below, Donna asked Elizabeth to stop the car so that she could take a photograph.

'Donna's a wunnerful photographer,' Hugh told Elizabeth. 'That's how we met. She'd taken pictures for one of my clients. Bill Brock, great guy. He's in the building business like my dad was, but on a massive scale.'

Evidently Donna hadn't found Glenmore Farm or its inhabitants to be photogenic. Although, Peggy thought, smiling grimly to herself, the last thing she wanted was to be photographed as she went about her everyday duties.

'The light is lovely in the evenings,' Elizabeth said to Donna. 'And it never gets properly dark here at this time of year.'

'You're kidding me!' For the first time Donna seemed impressed with something Scotland had to offer. She turned to look at Elizabeth. 'And you're really a farmer, like Hughie's uncle?'

'I manage the farm on the Rosland estate,' Elizabeth said. 'I was brought up on a farm — my dad was a shepherd. It's in my blood, I suppose.'

'I couldn't do it,' Donna shuddered. 'All those big animals. Besides, I gave up work the day I became Mrs Hugh Mackay.' She turned to give Hugh a flirtatious look.

Peggy caught Elizabeth's eye in the rear view mirror. She wondered if her cousin, like herself, felt both scornful and envious of Donna's last statement.

'Here you are, Peg.' Elizabeth drew up at the dairyman's house. 'Come over to the farmhouse when you're finished with June. Tibbie will be there of course if we're not back.'

'Was that Mrs Duncan's car?' June asked.

Peggy explained about the American visitors. 'I took the opportunity to come down to give you the script of *For Love or Money*,' she said. She held it out to June. 'I had a quick reread of it earlier,' she said. 'You've got a lot of lines.'

'I've got a good memory!' June said. 'And Tam says he'll hear me.'

'That's nice of him,' said Peggy. 'And we'll have lots of rehearsals. I really want Rosland WRI to do well. We've been placed in the competition under every president we've had. I've a reputation to keep up.'

'I won't let you down, Mrs Mackay.' June cocked her head to one side. 'Was that Sadie?' She half got to her feet and then sat down again. 'No, I don't think so.'

'Call me Peggy, please,' Peggy said. 'Where's Tam tonight?'

June made a face. 'Frank next door seemed to be at a loose end for once. Asked Tam if he'd go with him to the Rosland Inn for a game of darts. He wasn't keen — he's a home bird, my Tam — but he didn't like to be unfriendly.'

Frank Robertson must have been at a loose end, Peggy thought. It wasn't usually male company he sought out.

'How are you getting on with Isa?' she asked. 'She's not the most congenial neighbour, I'm afraid.'

'You're right there. I'm not going to repeat anything she's said to me. That woman has a mind like a midden. And yet,' June shrugged, 'she can be quite kind. She makes a fuss of Sadie. And she's asked me to go in sometime and watch the new television set Frank's bought for her. He's a good son, I'll say that for him.' June stood up. 'Would you like a cup of tea, Mrs ... Peggy?'

'No, thank you,' said Peggy, standing up herself. 'I'm going over to the farm-house. Elizabeth will give us a lift back up the road.'

'You're quite a way up in the hills, aren't you?' June said. 'You never learned to drive yourself?'

'No.' Peggy looked away for a moment. 'Well, my dear, I'll see you at the first play rehearsal — not till September so you've plenty of time to learn your lines.'

As she walked through the farmstead and up the road to Elizabeth's house Peggy's thoughts were dragged unwill-ingly backwards to that dreadful day, twenty years earlier, in 1943.

She was stepping out then with Dr Munro's son and, without permission, he'd borrowed his father's car — the doctor had petrol during that time of rationing. Peggy had been having a driv-ing lesson when the local bobby caught up with them. In a panic, she'd braked hard, and her erstwhile beau had hit his head on the dashboard and suffered mild concussion.

The whole thing got hushed up and it was the end of her romantic relationship with the doctor's son — not that that mattered because a few months later she met Alec. But not since that day had she been behind the wheel. Alec had never held it against her, that she couldn't drive, but she knew it would be useful in all sorts of ways if she could.

Now, as she passed Elizabeth's parked car, she thought — twenty years. It was a long time to be afraid of something.

20

June's heart sank.

She'd heard Isa's door slam shut and now there was a knock at her own door — which was half open this sunny morning, advertising the fact that June was there.

'Good morning, Isa.' It was in June's nature to be open and friendly and she smiled instinctively at the small woman with the perpetually sour expression, while at the same time determined not to let her come further than the doorstep. She knew from experience that Isa would stay all morning.

Her neighbour took the wind out of her sails by thrusting a little cardigan at her, knitted in light green wool. She brushed aside June's thanks. 'I can see you're busy now,' she said pointedly. 'Can you come round later to watch my television?'

Feeling guilty, June found herself agreeing.

The cardigan was soft and well-knitted but smelt of cigarette smoke. She'd have to wash it before it went anywhere near the baby.

Carrying Sadie, wearing a smocked summer dress and one of the many pink matinee jackets sent up by her mum from Paisley, June left it as long as possible before going next door.

'There's a bairns' programme on, you've almost missed it.' Isa greeted them. She looked at Sadie, her eyes narrowing. 'Pink! And her a redhead!'

I have to live beside this woman, June told herself, swallowing hard. *There isn't anything I can do about it.* She sat down on the sofa. Like the green cardigan, the room smelt of nicotine, and of past meals. Did Isa never open a window?

'Look, Sadie, that's Andy Pandy,' Isa said, pointing to the television screen where a puppet was climbing out of a picnic basket.

At the age of five months Sadie was

more interested in pulling her mother's hair.

Isa looked disappointed. 'I thought she'd like it.'

June felt guilty again. 'When she's a wee bit older, I'm sure she will.' She racked her brains trying to find some safe topic of conversation.

'Have you seen yon car Elizabeth Duncan's sister's driving?' Isa asked eagerly, before June could think of anything to say. 'As pink as the bairn's cardigan. I never saw the like. How did she pay for it? It must have cost a pretty penny. They say she's been modelling for a magazine. Modelling! Who does she think she is? But they'll not hear a word against her — not Elizabeth nor Tibbie Duncan. Tibbie! She's no need to put on airs and graces with me. I kent her faither! And if Christine, or whatever fancy name she calls herself, thinks that Dr Scott is keeping his own company while she's in London, well, let me tell you ... '

'How is Frank?' interrupted June desperately.

'He's down in the dumps because his lassie and her family moved away,' Isa said.

One of his lassies, thought June. But maybe that's why he'd sought out Tam's company the other night.

'He can do better for himself, anyway. He's going places, Frank is.' The honeyed tone Isa had adopted while talking about her son changed back to the gleeful one she used when imparting gossip. 'And Matthew Duncan.' She tapped the side of her nose.

June knew what was coming. It was one of the first stories Isa had told her. The last thing June wanted was to hear it again but there was no stopping the tide of words.

'What was he doing on the road there, that afternoon? I was in the farmyard myself when they came to give Elizabeth the news that he'd fallen off his horse. Why was he there? she says. I thought he was up on the hill.' Isa raised her eyebrows and nodded at June. 'I can guess what he was doing. I know whose house was near, who he must have been visiting.'

June felt sick. She'd hadn't known Matthew Duncan, of course, but she'd never heard anyone else say anything against him. And she liked and respected Elizabeth, who'd been very good to Tam and herself. Even listening to this sorry tale seemed a betrayal of Tam's boss.

'I'm not interested in gossip,' she said firmly. 'I don't think you should be talking like this, Isa.'

'Oh, don't you?' Isa stood up and put her hands on her hips. 'Well, you might not have to put up with me for much longer, madam.'

'What do you mean?'

'Lady Muck. Selling the estate, isn't she?' Isa said, her expression triumphant. 'We'll all be out on our ears by Christmas.'

Surely Tam would have heard a rumour if the estate was to be sold, June thought, as she set the table for their evening meal.

When he came home, he had a wash and then sat with Sadie on his knee. June handed him the day's post and prepared to tell him about her visit to Isa.

But Tam opened a letter which drove all other thoughts out of her head. It was from his auntie — Rita's mother. Rita had a new boyfriend, apparently, a more reliable one this time. It looked as if they might settle down together. She knew she'd given up her right to be Sadie's mum but, wrote auntie, Rita was wondering if Tam could send her a photograph of her baby.

21

'Doesn't one of Alec Mackay's lads owe us two days' work?' Rodney Shaw's grey, clipped moustache bristled with anger. 'That was the understanding, wasn't it, for the loan of our baler?'

'One them sprained his ankle,' Elizabeth said. She crossed her fingers behind her back. 'He'll be better by corn harvest time.'

Mr Shaw made a harrumphing noise. 'Don't go making these kind of arrangements again, Mrs Duncan. If Mackay can't afford a baler it's nothing to do with the estate. He's taking advantage of you because you're related to his wife.'

'He didn't ask. I offered,' said Elizabeth coldly, prepared to argue the matter, but the factor moved on. He shuffled papers on his desk as he said, 'When I was doing my rounds this morning it seemed to me that that prize bull of yours was limping.

Were you aware of that?'

'Tam hasn't said anything. I'll investigate. Is that everything, Mr Shaw?' Elizabeth couldn't wait to leave his office.

He didn't look up. 'Shut the door behind you.'

Tam Morrison looked concerned when Elizabeth sought him out. 'I haven't seen the bull this morning yet,' he said. 'I'll come with you to the field.'

The bull had been purchased by Lord Mannering on Matthew's advice, and had cost a great deal of money. So Elizabeth was extremely dismayed to see that the fine animal her husband had nicknamed Bonny Boy was indeed limping.

'What's the matter with him, do you think?' she asked Tam. 'Has he stood on something?'

The dairyman scanned the field. 'Lucky he's in by himself if that's the case. You set Jimmie to mend the barbed wire fence yesterday. He wouldn't have dropped some, would he?'

'He would be mending it from this

side. There was no reason for him to go into the field,' Elizabeth said. 'All right, Tam, you get on with your work. I'll phone the vet. I'll let you know when he comes. It will take the three of us to get Bonny Boy into a pen so Andy can examine him.'

Bonny Boy was generally quite docile, but today he was two and a half thousand pounds of angry Ayrshire bull. He allowed Andy Kerr to thread a chain through the steel ring in his nose and to clip it around the base of his horns but when it came to walking to the pen he refused to co-operate.

'I'm going to put on another chain,' Andy said, suiting actions to his words. 'Take one each and hold him steady. We'll see if he lets me close enough to have a look.'

Elizabeth was within inches of Bonny Boy's red-brown and white face. His large eyes were usually benign but now had a malevolent stare. She could see the sheen of sweat on Tam's forehead and felt it on her own. I'm doing this for Matthew, she thought, gripping onto the chain, unable to spare a hand to wipe her face.

'It's a deep cut,' Andy said. 'It needs stitches — we're going to have to get him into that pen.'

'Come on, Boy,' Elizabeth urged. 'Shall we try leading him again, Tam?'

Andy slapped the bull on his flank and this time Bonny Boy moved forward, but as Andy moved to shut the gate of the pen he suddenly roared and kicked out with his back leg, catching the vet off guard. Tam moved quickly and slammed home the bolt.

Elizabeth knelt by Andy. His eyes were closed. 'Are you all right?' She leaned over him and put her ear on his chest. His heart was thumping. Relieved, she sat up.

Andy's eyelids fluttered open. He tried to pull himself up. 'Ouch. Should have seen that coming.' He moved his hands carefully down his torso. 'I think he's just winded me. No broken bones.'

Elizabeth and Tam helped him up.

'I'll get my bag and do those stitches,' Andy said. He swayed a little on his feet.

'You're in no fit state to do anything,' said Elizabeth, torn between taking care of him and worrying about Bonny Boy.

'I reckon I could do it,' Tam said. 'If you give me guidance, Mr Kerr.'

'Could you, Tam?' said Elizabeth thankfully. She watched in trepidation as Tam gently lifted the afflicted hoof.

'It's deep alright,' he said. 'Looks like he stood on something sharp.' He raised his head to look at Elizabeth. 'Like barbed wire.'

Elizabeth insisted on driving Andy home in his car while Tam followed in her own.

Together they helped him into his house. Elizabeth had never been in it before, the house Andy had been brought up in, and where he now lived on his own. It was clean and tidy but somehow comfortless, a bachelor establishment.

'I'm going to phone your colleague, tell him to take over from you today,' she told Andy. 'You've had a shock,' she said as Andy protested.

'Occupational hazard of being a vet, a

beast's hind leg.' Andy lifted his own legs cautiously onto the sofa.

'And I'm going to pop into the surgery on the way home, get Dr Scott to come and look at you,' Elizabeth went on.

'No need for that,' Andy said. 'I can tell nothing's broken.'

'I feel responsible,' Elizabeth said. 'I'd like him to check you over.'

There was a now-familiar pink Mini outside the doctor's. Elizabeth looked at her watch. The doctor would be finishing morning surgery and about to start his house calls. It was an odd time for Crys to be there.

As she got out of the car the door of the surgery opened and Crys came running out. Elizabeth could see that she'd been crying. Struan Scott stood in the doorway for a moment then went back inside.

Elizabeth held out her arms to her sister. 'What's happened?'

'He's getting married,' Crys wailed. 'He's had a fiancée all along!'

'Shall we go for a walk? It's such a lovely

afternoon,' Mamie asked Neil.

He put his pipe in his pocket. 'If you promise not to run on ahead of a shuffling old man.'

Mamie tucked her arm through his. 'The doctor — the doctor said gentle strolls would be good for your back.'

At the mention of the doctor, Neil's face darkened. Mamie berated herself for mentioning him. Bad back or no bad back, Neil had been all for going down to the surgery and having it out with Struan Scott for playing fast and loose with his daughter's feelings.

Through her storms of tears Crys had begged him not to. And Mamie weighed in too. 'Crys is grown-up. She knows you're upset on her behalf, we both are. But there's nothing you can do that won't make things worse.' Eventually Neil had calmed down.

Now Mamie said as they turned off the tarred road and along a grassy track, 'We won't have to see him for much longer. His six months here will be up soon. Poor Crys. She fell very hard for him.'

'Always thought he was smarmy,' Neil growled.

Mamie squeezed his arm against hers in non-committal response. She knew that Neil's opinion of Struan was only in retrospect — they'd both found him personable, and believed him to be honest, up until the moment when Crys, having got wind of a rumour that he was engaged to someone back in his hometown, had gone to confront him and come back distraught.

Both their girls were going through the mill at the moment, Mamie reflected. Crys had driven away in the strawberry-pink Mini that eventful day last week and was now in London 'throwing myself into work' as she put it, and apparently taking advantage of her school chum Robbie MacLean's good nature by crying on his shoulder.

And Elizabeth — on top of her ongoing tussle of wills with the factor, Rodney Shaw, she had the worry of the accident that had happened to the estate's prize bull. Fortunately, his cut hoof was on the mend and the vet, Andy Kerr, had recovered from being kicked in his middle, but the whole incident was upsetting.

Mamie had no doubt that Elizabeth was more than capable of managing the estate's Home Farm. But it took its toll — it was a seven-day-week job, a heap of form-filling to do as well as the outside work. All that didn't leave her much time to spend with her little daughters. Her mother-in-law Tibbie was a rock she could lean on but wasn't the easiest person to live with — her presence, too, was a constant reminder that Matthew was gone.

Two years now since Elizabeth's husband's fatal accident. Mamie was proud of the way her daughter had coped, emotionally as well as practically. It would be nice, though, if she had someone to share her burdens with — had Elizabeth ever considered that she might get married again, Mamie wondered? She still wore her wedding ring, a signal that she still felt married to Matthew. But then she never met anyone new. Her world was her work and her girls. There was no time or opportunity for anything else.

'Penny for them.' Neil nudged her.

'Oh.' Mamie gave a sigh and a laugh. 'Not sure they're worth that much. Before I had children I never thought that you would always worry about them, no matter how old they were.'

'Aye, it's a job for life, right enough.' Neil stopped. 'Here's a boulder. Let's have a sit-down for a minute.

'Crys will get over it. Plenty more fish … ' he said, putting his arm around Mamie's shoulders.

Mamie nodded. She wouldn't say that it hadn't been Crys she'd been thinking of. Matthew had been the son they'd never had — he and Neil had been great friends as well as in-laws. She didn't want to say to Neil that her mind had leaped ahead to a time when Elizabeth might fall in love with someone else.

But there was a piece of family news she could impart although she'd have to swear him to secrecy. Peggy didn't want anyone else to know but it would be impossible to keep from Neil.

'Don't tell a soul what I'm about to tell you. Promise,' she said.

Neil crossed his heart. 'Hope it's nothing illegal.'

'Don't be daft. Well. You may have noticed that I got a letter from Peggy this morning?'

'And?' As Glenmore Farm wasn't on the phone, a letter from Peggy was a frequent occurrence. 'Nothing wrong, I hope?'

'She — wants — me,' Mamie said slowly, spinning out the information, 'to — give — her — driving lessons!'

She saw with satisfaction that she had succeeded in surprising him.

Neil whistled. 'Alec told me the story of her and old Dr Munro's son. I can see why that would put her off learning. What's brought this on now?'

'Not sure really. She says it would be a help to Alec and of course it would. But that's always been the case. I think she's just decided at last to face her fears over it.'

144

'But why you?' Neil asked.

'Well, obviously, you don't ask your husband to teach you to drive, do you?' Mamie smiled sweetly at him. 'That's a recipe for disaster and the divorce courts, as you and I nearly found out.'

Neil grinned back. 'I remember.'

'Anyway, she doesn't want Alec to know — I think she imagines herself flourishing her driving licence at him. Besides, we're out of the way here and there's the old war aerodrome over the hill — that will be a grand place to practise in secret.'

'And how's she going to explain to Alec why she's coming over here so often?'

'That will be tricky. Depends how she gets on. Maybe we'll only go out the once, who knows. But I thought — that box of recipe cuttings I've got. There are hundreds. She can say she's helping me sort them out.'

'But you said you were looking forward to doing that yourself.'

'I am, and I will. But Alec doesn't know that.'

'Very devious. So when is this first lesson to be?'

'Hugh and his wife have gone now, to the Western Isles, but they're coming back in August for a few days — for the agricultural show. Alec will be getting his animals ready for the judging soon. Then it will be harvest time,' said Mamie. 'Peg will be kept busy on the farm. We'll have to wait until after that.'

22

June knew that Tam worried for days over the request from his aunt for a photograph of baby Sadie. She didn't know how to respond to it either. She didn't even want to think about it. It was the first contact they'd had with his aunt, whose daughter Rita was Sadie's natural mother, since the baby had been handed over to Tam and June almost six months earlier.

Tam brought the subject up once more as he and June sat on the sofa listening to the wireless after their evening meal.

'We can't refuse to do it, can we?' He seemed to be thinking aloud, not expecting June to answer. 'That would be unkind, maybe cause bad feeling in the family too.'

'It would be like giving Sadie back to Rita in some way,' June burst out. 'I'm sorry, I know that doesn't make sense but that's how I feel.'

'So you don't want to do it?' Tam rubbed his hand over his forehead.

'No, I don't.' June leaned her head against his shoulder. 'But of course we must. Sadie's legally ours but she's part of Rita, she's your aunt's granddaughter.'

'You're right. Nothing can change that.'

'It's just a photo,' June said, trying to believe it. 'A wee piece of shiny paper. We have the real live Sadie.'

Tam took June's hand. 'We do. When you think of it that way, it's not too much to ask, is it?'

'There are some snaps in the camera, aren't there?' asked June. 'Next time we're in town we can hand them in to be developed.'

Tam shook his head. 'No — well, yes there are and I got to the end of the film,' he said. 'But, you're in all of them too, Junie. There aren't any of Sadie on her own. I don't know what you think of this idea —' He hesitated. 'We could go and have a picture professionally taken. There's a studio in town.'

June considered the matter. 'That is a good idea. If we're going to do it we should do it properly. And maybe we could get one of the three of us at the same time, you, me and Sadie? We could have it framed and put it on the mantelpiece.'

'That's an even better idea.' Tam planted a kiss on her cheek. 'I'll go and look out the camera now and we can nip into town tomorrow morning after milking. Take our film in for developing and go to the studio. Best get dressed in our finery in case they can take us right away!'

'I was wondering.' It was June's turn to hesitate. 'Do you think we could go to the manse on the way home? I'd like to ask about having Sadie christened.'

They hadn't been big church-goers back home but they'd gone to the Rosland village church a few times. On the first occasion Sadie had got noisy and June took her out — which proved to be an ice-breaker. Everyone had seen them and came up afterwards to say hello and admire the red-haired baby.

'What's brought this on?' Tam asked.

'I thought it would be something good to do for Sadie. And maybe make us feel that this is where we belong now, the three of us.'

Tam could have brought up the rumour, passed to June by her spiteful next-door neighbour, Isa, that Lady Annabel was selling the estate and they'd all have to leave. But he didn't. He kissed June again. 'I like that. Let's do it.'

Peggy leant her bike against the shop wall. The window was half-covered with a poster for the agricultural show. Peering around it, she could see that Nancy had one customer, Isa Robertson. Peggy certainly didn't want to go in while she was there. She lurked away from the window until Isa emerged.

'Morning, Isa.'

If Peggy had hoped that she'd get away with merely a greeting she was to be disappointed. Isa came over. 'Your Americans gone? I heard Alec put them to work. A slave-driver, like his father before him, by all accounts.'

Even Alec's father would have been pushed to get Donna working on the farm. The thought of those red-tipped hands stacking hay or mucking out the byre made Peggy smile. But the work Hugh had done, he'd done happily and at his own insistence.

'Well, maybe that's what you heard,' she said. There was no point in arguing with the woman. 'Now excuse me, the slave-driver has given me some time off this morning.' She walked past Isa and once inside the shop closed the door loudly behind her.

She'd get her bit of business over first before she did her grocery shopping.

Standing at the Post Office counter, she dived straight in before Nancy could start a leisurely chat.

'I'd like —' She took a deep breath. ' — a form to get a provisional driving licence.'

'Colin taking his test soon?' Nancy made no move to get the form. 'Your boys have been driving in the field for years, haven't they? Going to make it official?'

For a moment Peggy was tempted to go along with that. It would be a little white lie maybe, hardly a lie at all. She could let Nancy think the form was for Colin — he would be seventeen on his next birthday after all.

But Nancy was one of her longest-standing friends and although she liked knowing what was going on and spreading any news, she could be relied on to keep a secret.

'Actually, it's for me,' Peggy said. 'Don't say anything, Nance. Auntie Mamie's going to give me lessons. Alec knows nothing about it.'

'Well! That's a surprise.' As Nancy reached into one of the pigeonholes behind her for the form, the door jangled open. 'It'll be one in the eye for that man of yours when you tell him you've passed your test.'

Peggy turned round to see who'd come in. Isa.

Nancy paused, the form hovering between herself and Peggy.

'Did I leave my umbrella in here?' Isa asked, looking from one to the other.

How much had she overheard?

Nancy handed Peggy the form. 'Tell Colin good luck from me,' she said, giving Peggy a tiny wink. 'Isa, I haven't seen an umbrella. Yours or anyone else's.'

Isa left, grumbling under her breath.

'Umbrella, my foot,' Nancy said. 'There's not been a cloud in the sky for two days. An excuse to overhear us, if you ask me.'

Peggy pushed the form to the bottom of her shopping bag, a new problem just occurring to her. 'Can I get the licence sent here, care of the Post Office?' she asked. 'Otherwise Alec might see it.'

"What a tangled web we weave",' quoted Nancy. 'Course you can. I can't think who'd be a more patient teacher than Mamie.'

'I hope I don't try her patience too much,' Peggy sighed. She hoped, actually, that she wasn't going to have second thoughts about the whole thing.

23

It wasn't a conversation Elizabeth had looked forward to having.

She'd asked Tam to send Jimmie to her office. The farmhand — a reliable worker who'd never quite grown up — came in, twisting his cap between his hands.

After the accident, when Bonny Boy was still safely in the pen, Tam had walked over the field and found pieces of the sharp wire scattered about on the grass. But when Elizabeth questioned Jimmie about the repairs to the barbed wire fence he maintained that he'd done as she'd asked — mended the fence without going into the field, and taken the unused wire back to the shed.

When he began to get upset she changed the subject and asked if he would help Tam nearer the time with grooming the cows they'd send for judging at the agricultural show. She knew that working with animals was what he liked best.

Now, a week after the accident, the cut was on the mend, thank goodness, and, after a couple of days' rest, the vet, Andy Kerr, was back to work. She couldn't help thinking that he'd made light of the blow he'd received.

On impulse she lifted the phone. 'Andy? Elizabeth. How are you?'

'It'll take more than your Bonny Boy to put me out of business,' Andy laughed.

'It's good to hear you — you do sound all right. I've been worried … look, I was wondering if you were free this evening to come and eat with us? I'm not sure what Tibbie's planning to have but there's always enough for an army.'

'Let me check my diary. No. No other invitations.' She could hear the grin in his voice.

'Good. We eat early of course because of the girls — six o' clock?'

'I'll be there.'

'There's a letter for you, from London.'

Tibbie handed Elizabeth an envelope covered in her sister's rounded handwriting.

Elizabeth looked at the clock. Ten to six. She'd managed a wash and changed into a summer dress. Tibbie had set an extra place at the table. Everything was in hand.

'I'll just have a quick read, if there's nothing you want me to do.' She ripped the envelope open.

Struan phoned, wrote Crys. *His fiancée has heard about me and broken off their engagement. He says he loves me, wants me to come home and start again. I'm crazy about him but how can I trust him? What should I do? Don't tell Mum and Dad, I know what they'd say.*

'There's Andy now,' said Tibbie from the window.

Elizabeth pushed the letter back in the envelope. She'd read the rest later. Yes, she thought, Mum and Dad would say have nothing to do with him. You're young. You'll meet someone else. Plenty more fish in the sea. Her instinct was to agree with them. Perhaps Struan had genuine feelings for Crystal but he should have extricated himself from one relationship before embarking on another. Elizabeth and her parents would find it hard to forgive him for that.

But it had to be Crys's decision. It was her life. How could anyone advise her what to do?

Andy came in looking slightly self-conscious. He had a box of chocolates in his hand, a large one with roses on the lid, and looked undecided as to whether to hand it to Elizabeth or to Tibbie. The matter was decided for him when he saw the longing gazes directed on the box by Elizabeth's little girls, Libby and Flora. With a laugh he handed it over.

'You're not to open it now,' Tibbie warned them, predictably.

'You can have one each, if you finish all your tea.' Elizabeth softened the blow of Tibbie's words. 'Andy, come and sit down.'

Tibbie had made a high tea of cold

ham, salad and fried potatoes, followed by scones and fruitcake. She looked benignly on Andy as he tucked in.

'It's grand to get some home cooking.' He nodded his thanks.

He was the only person who really appreciated Tibbie's rather heavy scones and cake, Elizabeth thought, hiding a smile. It was a pity he had no one at home to look after him. A thought began to cross her mind but before she could explore it further Tibbie said to Andy, 'That was a bad knock you got. I mind it happened to my late husband once — cow kicked him in the shin. He was laid up for weeks.'

'I didn't know he was a farm worker, Mrs Duncan.'

'He was a stonemason,' Tibbie said, 'but he used to help his brother out on the family farm. What a mess his leg was in. Matthew — Matthew was a wee boy at the time. He was sitting on the gate, saw it happening.'

There was a pause.

'It didn't put Matthew off then?' Andy

asked. 'He still wanted to work on a farm himself.'

Tibbie nodded. She was looking a little white around the mouth, as she always did at the mention of Matthew, her only child.

'Flora, eat up,' Elizabeth said, more sharply than she intended, to change the subject

'Shan't.' It was Flora's favourite word this week.

'Come on.' Elizabeth picked up Flora's fork and speared a piece of potato. 'Here, have one for baby Sadie. And one for Tomcat up at Glenmore ... when they're all finished you can have a chocolate.'

'I don't believe in bribing children to eat.' Tibbie sniffed her disapproval as she pushed her chair back and stood up. 'I'll make a pot of tea.'

Libby looked shyly at Andy. 'Can we do a jigsaw again?'

'Andy won't want ... ' Elizabeth began.

'I'd like to,' Andy said, 'really, I would.'

Elizabeth nodded to Libby. 'All right, but take your plate through to the kitchen first.' She popped another fried potato slice into Flora's mouth.

'Come to any conclusions about what happened to Bonny Boy, about the barbed wire?' Andy asked.

Elizabeth wondered if she should say anything to Andy about the strands of wire Tam had found. She'd had to tell Rodney Shaw of course and he'd advised her not to talk about it, said he would make his own enquiries.

But she told Andy about her talk with Jimmie. 'I believe him,' she said. 'He's always been truthful and he loves animals. He'd never do anything that would harm them.'

'It was Rodney Shaw who first saw Bonny Boy limping?'

'Yes.' Elizabeth wondered if he'd told Lady Annabel. She was afraid of where Shaw's 'enquiries' would take him. Jimmie would be his first suspect and an easy target for his bullying questions.

'You don't think maybe ... ' Andy stopped. 'No, even he ... '

'What? You think Rodney Shaw had

something to do with it?' Elizabeth clattered the fork down onto Flora's plate.

'No, forget it,' Andy said. 'Stupid idea.' He reached for another piece of fruitcake. 'How's Crys? I heard it all ended in tears with Dr Scott.'

Elizabeth looked at him. The thought that had begun to cross her mind earlier returned. Andy was a few years older than Crys, certainly, but so what? Dad was right. It was time her scatty little sister settled down. Andy was unmarried, a nice, steady man, good with children. The next time Crys was home she'd ask her and Andy here together.

'She's upset but she'll get over it,' she said.

Libby came back with a jigsaw and Elizabeth began to clear the table so the pieces could be spread out.

The more she thought about it the better the idea seemed. Life was like a series of jigsaws really. Sometimes a piece was irretrievably lost, as in her own case.

But you could try to join other pieces together to make a satisfying picture. Yes, she would do some matchmaking. Her sister and their childhood friend. Why hadn't she thought of it before?

24

A photograph of Sadie had gone down to Paisley, to Tam's aunt. Sadie was so adorable in it, lying on her tummy on a blanket and smiling right at the camera, that Tam and June had ordered a copy of it for themselves, as well as the photograph of the three of them. Both, now framed, were added to the mantelpiece in the front room to sit beside their wedding photo, and one of them taken last Christmas with June's family.

June was dusting the mantelpiece and gloating over the pictures again when she heard Isa's door bang shut.

When the visit to watch television next door had ended on a very sour note, with June telling Isa she didn't want to hear any unpleasant tittle-tattle about their neighbours, June had thought — hoped, if truth be told — that Isa would stop speaking to her altogether.

But Isa acted as though nothing had happened — perhaps because June was right next door she was a captive audience that Isa was not going to let go. A few days after that visit Isa had handed in a little jumper for Sadie that had a picture of Andy Pandy knitted into the front. Much as she would have liked to break contact, June didn't have the heart to refuse the gift Isa had clearly gone to a lot of trouble to make.

Now, as she heard a knock at her own door, she knew it must be Isa. She looked at Sadie propped up on cushions in her playpen — and wearing the Andy Pandy jumper. That should put Isa in a good mood.

But when she came in, and June put the kettle on for morning coffee, Isa only seemed to have one subject on her mind. Her son Frank.

'He's been like a bear with a sore paw, this past week or so. I can't get a civil word out of him.'

'Didn't you say his girlfriend had moved away with her family?'

'It's not that,' Isa scoffed. 'Frank's never been one to be upset over a lassie for long. It's always the other way — many's a time I've opened my door to find some girl in tears asking for him.'

June spooned coffee into cups. 'So what do you think is wrong?' It was a question she would put to anyone in the circumstances but asking Isa anything felt like she was conspiring with her in some nefarious gossip. She didn't really want to know the answer.

'I think Rodney Shaw's been getting at him again. I saw them having an argument in the farmyard but I couldn't hear what it was about and Frank wouldn't say.'

June wasn't going to tell Isa that Tam thought Rodney Shaw was a nasty piece of work. But she had often seen with her own eyes Frank going off somewhere, all dressed up, when he should have been working — so the factor had every right to be angry with him if he found out.

'I hope no one's been telling tales.' Isa gave June a beady stare over the top of her cup. 'Frank's a hard worker. He's entitled to a bit of fun.'

June had heard it all before. I'm going to stop this conversation now, she thought. 'Look,' she said, smiling over at the playpen. 'Sadie loves her new jumper.'

Isa's expression softened. 'I wanted a wee girl after Frank. But it wasn't to be.'

June had a moment of fellow-feeling with her difficult neighbour. 'We had a lovely photo taken of Sadie. Would you like to see it?' she asked, scooping Sadie up and blowing a raspberry into her neck. 'Shall we show Isa you lying on that furry blanket?' She led the way through to the front room.

Isa admired the two new photographs and then peered closely at the wedding picture. 'How long have you been married?'

'Five years.' Already June was regretting taking Isa through their house, telling her anything.

'And when was this one taken?' Isa picked up the fourth photograph and stared at it. 'Is that your mother? You look like her.'

'Yes, it is — last Christmas,' June said, 'at my mum and dad's.'

'Last Christmas,' Isa repeated. She looked puzzled. 'But —' Evidently she changed her mind about saying more, but clearly something had made her think.

It was only later, when June was giving Sadie her last bottle of the evening, the baby's trustful blue eyes fixed on hers, that she realised what that something could be.

Last Christmas was just six weeks before Sadie was born. But in the photo there was June in her best dress, cinched in at the waist, clearly not about to have a baby.

Her heart sank. What was Isa going to make of that piece of information?

25

Diffidently, Tam had asked Elizabeth if the rumours about Lady Annabel selling up were true.

'You got this from Isa, I suppose?' Elizabeth asked.

Tam nodded. 'I know she talks a lot of blethers but ... no smoke without fire as they say.'

Elizabeth had gathered that day in Rosland House that Lady Annabel was concerned about the future of all her properties. But she replied to Tam saying truthfully that if selling Rosland was her Ladyship's plan she had not told her farm manager.

Tam's worried face had cleared. 'Good to hear that, Mrs Duncan. June and me wouldn't want to upsticks again so soon.'

'Believe me, Tam. If there's anything I think my staff should know I will tell them.'

A couple of weeks after that conversation Elizabeth wondered if she knew anything at all about what was happening on the estate. Lady Annabel had been closeted in Rodney Shaw's office several times, with the door firmly shut. The mystery of Bonny Boy's injury remained just that, a mystery. If Rodney Shaw had made enquiries he never reported any results to Elizabeth.

And the men were saying that Shaw and Frank Robertson had almost come to blows the other day — and while there had always bad feeling between them it had never descended so far before. No one seemed to know what they'd argued over.

On the bright side, Andy had taken to calling in at the farmhouse and asking if he could do anything for them. Tibbie had asked him to cut some kindling sticks, and move a wardrobe from one room to another. Elizabeth was grateful — Tibbie wasn't up to chopping wood anymore and she herself hadn't enough hours in the day.

There were things she could call on the estate to do — sort the leak in the roof, mend the shed door, because the house and the shed were estate property — but she didn't want to ask any of the men for help with more personal chores. She wanted to show that she could cope with managing the farm, and with everything else.

Sometimes she found herself thinking about Donna Mackay and her life in California. What must it be like not to have to think about anything apart from which colour to paint your nails?

But her matchmaking plans were off to a good start. Andy had stayed to eat with them again, and Elizabeth had come downstairs one evening after supervising the girls' bath-time to find him drying the dishes for Tibbie.

Good. It would perfectly natural then for him to be there when Crystal was home. She began dropping Crys's name into conversation whenever she could, and she read snippets of her letters that could be shared.

'Crys isn't coming home for the agricultural show,' she told him one afternoon in her office. He wasn't over for a social call this time but to check up on Bonny Boy's hoof. 'She wouldn't have anyway, because she doesn't want to run into Struan Scott, but she's got a lot of work — modelling bridal gowns, of all things, in a department store in Oxford Street. She used to love the show, she's sorry to miss it.'

'Wasn't there some story about her and candyfloss?' Andy chuckled.

'It was the first year there was a candyfloss stall.' Elizabeth laughed at the memory. 'Dad gave her some money and she went straight over and spent the lot! Six sticks. She had all this pink fluff — '

The door opened, banging against the wall, and Tibbie almost ran in, clutching Libby by the hand.

'What is it?' Elizabeth stood up, her heart beating fast. Tibbie never came to the estate office. 'What's wrong?'

'Flora was playing with her dolly in

the garden,' Tibbie gasped. 'But she's not now. I've looked all around and called and called. I can't find her anywhere.'

26

June put a sleeping Sadie in her pram and lifted it carefully over the backdoor step. She pulled the hood up and fixed a net in front of it in case of insects.

Today, she was going to paint their kitchen cabinet. Her mum had passed it on to them when they moved here and it needed smartening up. They'd bought a tin each of cream and green paint and she was looking forward to deciding where each colour would go.

She stirred the tin of cream paint first. The colour and the smell reminded her of the first house she and Tam had had in their married life. The farmer had been parsimonious and wouldn't pay for the much-needed redecoration of the dairyman's cottage so they'd done it themselves, green walls with cream woodwork. Here, at Rosland, all the buildings were well maintained and their house had been freshly painted inside for their arrival.

Both Tam and herself were fervently hoping that the rumour about Lady Annabel selling up wasn't true — or if it was, that the estate would be bought by someone who would keep all the staff on.

Propped up on the kitchen table was the script for the WRI drama *For Love or Money*. As June drew the brush up and down the doors of the cabinet she muttered her lines to herself. Peggy was right — she did have a lot to say but, with Tam's help over many evenings, she was almost there. His rendering of the other characters' lines to give June her prompts reduced them both to helpless laughter, but at the end of next month, September, the WRI would start up again and rehearsals would begin in earnest.

What with concentrating on the lines, and on giving the cabinet a neat finish, it was some time before she realised that Sadie must be awake. There were chirruping sounds coming from the pram — and a springy noise, as if someone was rocking the pram handle up and down.

'Tam? Is that you?'

There was no reply but the springy noise stopped. June laid the brush down carefully and crossed the kitchen to the back door.

Outside, holding on to the pram, was Mrs Duncan's youngest daughter, four-year-old Flora.

June looked around the back garden. There was no one else there. 'Flora! What are you doing here? Does your mummy or your granny know where you are?'

Flora shook her fair pigtails blithely. 'I walked all by myself.'

'Stay there. You can rock the pram again if you like.' Inside, June flew to the phone. The estate numbers were on a pad beside it. She dialled the farmhouse. No reply. She ran outside again.

'Would you like to push the pram, Flora?' she asked.

She removed the net, took down the hood and propped up Sadie, gummily smiling, on her pillow. 'Look, Sadie's pleased to see you,' she said, anxious to hold on to Flora until she delivered her safely back.

Flora steered the pram carefully round to the front of the house and out of the gate. Isa was in her front garden, bending down and pulling up weeds in a desultory fashion. She never usually showed much interest in how her garden looked so it was clearly an excuse to see what was going on. As June and Flora passed her gate, Isa stood up and put her hand to her back in an exaggerated fashion.

'Taking her home?' she asked.

June was going to pass by without a word but Flora stopped to beam at Isa. 'I'm pushing the pram.'

'I saw you going past a few minutes ago, you little madam. Did you run away from your granny?'

'I wanted to see the baby.' Flora turned back to the pram and was about to push it when her mother came running round the corner.

'Oh, thank goodness. You little monkey. You've given your granny and me a dreadful fright.' Elizabeth grabbed Flora and hugged her. 'You must never, never do that again. Promise?'

'A good spanking, that's what she needs,' Isa put in.

June could see Elizabeth literally biting her lip in an effort not to retort. 'Come into the house, Mrs Duncan. You're all out of breath.'

'I must tell my mother-in-law … '

'We can try the phone. She may have gone back home, to see if Flora's there.'

This time Tibbie answered and sounded very thankful when June told her Flora was safe and with her mother.

June took Sadie out of the pram and asked Flora if she'd like to hold her. But her mother decided that this was a treat Flora didn't deserve. 'No, not today, Flora. You've been a very naughty girl. I must get back to work — the vet's here to see Bonny Boy, or at least he was until he set off to look for you.' Elizabeth gestured towards the window. 'Is she still there?' she asked June, who peered out cautiously.

'Excitement's over,' she said. 'She must have gone inside.'

'I hope you don't believe everything she tells you,' Elizabeth said.

She wasn't the first person who'd said that. Obviously June was not going to repeat Isa's scandalous stories, some of which concerned Mrs Duncan's own family. But she thought she would take the opportunity to alert her to some gossip that Isa would likely be spreading about Tam and herself.

'Can I tell you something?' she asked. She laid Sadie on the floor and gave Flora a rattle to wave at her.

'You may hear some news about us, about Sadie,' she went on, hesitantly. 'I'd like to tell you myself rather than you get Isa's half-baked version.' She told Elizabeth briefly about the photograph Isa had seen that clearly showed June could not be Sadie's natural mother, and about the baby's adoption.

To her surprise, Elizabeth gave her a hug, saying fiercely, 'If I hear one word about this that I can trace back to Isa, I'll have something to say to her.'

But June shook her head. 'Do you know, I feel better for telling you. It was bound to come out sooner or later. So let Isa do her worst. She's a poor soul, really.'

'That's very generous. There's not many round here that would agree with you.' Elizabeth reached for Flora's hand and pulled her to her feet. 'I'm sorry you had your morning disrupted, June. Now, miss, let's get you home. I cannot imagine what Granny Tib is going to say to you.'

27

The house was ready for the second time for the American visitors.

Hugh's postcard had said that they were having a wonderful time exploring the Western Isles but were both looking forward to being back in Glenmore.

Hmm. Peggy took the sentiment with a large pinch of salt. No doubt Hugh would be pleased to see them again and he'd got childishly excited when Alec had told him about the agricultural show this Saturday. But as for Donna, well, Peggy knew what to expect from her this time and it wasn't Hugh's enthusiasm for the old family farm.

This afternoon, though, Peggy would actually be here when they arrived. She could almost laugh about it now, the scene that had met her on their first visit — Davy and his hurt ankle, Donna like an exotic flower in the farmhouse kitchen, and the ruins of her beautiful rhubarb tart.

She was taking no chances this time. Anything that Donna had vaguely expressed a liking for was on the menu tonight — cold roast chicken, a salad with the dressing recipe Mamie had given her, and a summer pudding with their own thick cream. It was all prepared and the pantry door was locked, the key in Peggy's apron pocket where marauding hungry boys wouldn't find it. The glistening jars of raspberry and rhubarb jam she'd made for the WRI tent at the Show were all in there too. Last year she'd got two third prizes. Maybe she'd do better this year.

She'd made up the bed in the guest bedroom and put a posy of flowers on the dressing table. Donna's dismissal of the room hadn't taken away Peggy's delight in the pretty wallpaper and new curtains. Perhaps, she thought charitably, you had to have seen the room before in all its ghastliness to appreciate it now.

Ever since Hugh and Donna had left for the islands, Colin, Peggy and Alec's first-born, had talked of nothing but California. Peggy was torn between not wanting to squash him and wishing he'd think of the effect his chatter was having on his father. If Colin left, could Glenmore be farmed by just Alec and Davy? She didn't dare ask. And what was going to happen when Hugh and Donna went home? Was Colin going to ask if he could go with them? Peggy knew nothing about the process of moving to another country — what would it cost for one thing? There must be forms to fill, a passport to be got.

She tried to close her mind to the subject. Sufficient unto the day is the evil thereof, her mother used to say. Don't worry about tomorrow, in other words. Easier said than done, though.

The bedroom over the porch was tidier than usual — both boys had always slept there but now Davy had become attached to the little room downstairs he'd been in since his accident and declared he'd stay there, even although his ankle was more or less recovered.

On the bedside cabinet, beside Colin's bed, was the book of souvenir postcards of California that Hugh had given them. So that's where it had gone. She picked it up and leafed through it. Blue sky, yellow sun, blue sea, yellow sand. It was all dazzling. And so far away.

Davy, being mostly confined to the house during Hugh's visit, had heard fewer tales of the wonders of America that got Colin all fired up. No talk about emigrating from him, Peggy thought thankfully as, downstairs, she tipped Tomcat off Davy's bed and pulled back the bedclothes. Out fell a crumpled piece of paper.

Her first instinct when she saw what was on it was to run and tell Alec. But he had enough on his plate today, getting ready for the Show. Besides, he must be thinking about Colin possibly disappearing off to pastures new. She couldn't land this on him now. And maybe it didn't mean Davy was actually thinking about … Maybe it was just a scrap of paper. She could ask Davy himself of course but he hadn't said anything so it would seem like prying.

She made the bed and replaced the paper under the quilt.

'Mummy! I want to go up there.' Flora pointed to the fairground part of the Show, where the gaily decorated swing boats carried their excited passengers back and forth.

'They're for big boys and girls,' Tibbie jumped in to reply, 'and cost too many pennies.'

Flora held out her palm. 'I've got pennies.' Elizabeth had given them six each to spend.

'Put them in your pocket. You'll lose them,' instructed her granny.

'Shall we go and find a ride for girls of six and four?' Elizabeth suggested quickly before Flora's mutinous expression was translated into words. 'Do you remember last year there was one with little cars?'

'Not cars.' Flora seemed very definite on that point.

'I remember,' Libby said. 'We liked them, Flora. You sat in the driver's seat.'

Flora brightened up. 'Can we drive in the car, Mummy?'

'I'll take them,' Elizabeth said to Tibbie. 'Why don't you go to the WRI tent and we'll join you there?'

'I'll come with you, Tibbie,' Peggy said. 'See if I got placed for my jam. Would you like to come, Donna?'

'What is this tent?' Donna lifted her right foot and twisted round to inspect the spiky heel of her white sandal, which had sunk into the grass.

'It's competitions,' Peggy explained. 'The ladies in the Rural — that's the Women's Rural Institute — put in their handicrafts and baking and jam. Tibbie always wins prizes for her knitting and sewing.'

Donna looked almost interested. 'Like a county fair at home? I'll check it out. I'll leave you to the cows, Hughie.'

'See you later, honey.' Hugh kissed his wife. 'Have fun.'

Alec's face seemed to be expressing relief that the womenfolk were leaving them in peace. 'I've got some old cronies who remember your father,' he said to Hugh.

'Really, Uncle Alec?' Hugh's face lit up. 'It would be so great to talk with them. Enjoy your car ride, girls.' He made to move away with Alec when a skirl of music made him turn round. 'Hey!' He shaded his eyes. 'Hang on there. It can't be …'

Elizabeth followed his gaze. Preceded by a piper, Lady Annabel and her house party were being shown to their seats in the covered stand.

'That's my employer, the estate owner,' Elizabeth said to Hugh. 'She always has guests up for fishing and shooting at this time of year.'

'That big guy, on the left,' Hugh said, pointing. 'I know him. Bill Brock — I think I mentioned him to you? He's responsible for my state of matrimony!' He put his hand on Alec's shoulder. 'I must find out what the heck he's doing here. Wanna come?'

Alec seemed less than enthusiastic. 'You go on, lad. I'll wait here.'

Hugh hesitated. Perhaps he was uncertain about approaching the stand, thinking there was some protocol he should follow.

'I'll come with you, introduce you,' Elizabeth said. She took Libby and Flora by the hand. 'You'll have a ride on the cars in a minute, girls. We're going to see those people over there. Answer nicely if they speak to you.'

But as they approached the stand the man caught sight of Hugh. He looked almost comically surprised, waved, and then leant across to say something to Lady Annabel before bounding down the steps.

'Hugh Mackay, you old son-of-a-gun!' He slapped Hugh on the back. 'How d'you come to be in this neck of the woods?' His accent mirrored Hugh's own.

Hugh returned the greeting. 'Meeting my wunnerful Scottish family, my dad's folks,' he said. He indicated Elizabeth. 'This is Elizabeth Duncan, my — well, a kind of cousin. She works for Lady

Annabel. Elizabeth, Bill Brock. Bill was one of my first clients. It was through him I met Donna.'

Elizabeth remembered the name and the story. Donna had been taking photographs for this man's construction company.

Bill Brock held out his hand, his smile crinkling his face. 'Good to meet you, kind-of-cousin.'

Elizabeth let go of Flora. 'How do you do.' She couldn't help noticing the colour of his eyes, somewhere between dark blue and gray.

'My name's Flora. I'm a cousin too,' Flora piped up.

Bill Brock crouched down. 'You've got a lovely name, Flora. Is this your sister?'

Libby nodded shyly.

'I'm four and Libby's six. She's at school. I'll go when I'm five. I ... '

'Flora. Stop being a chatterbox,' Elizabeth chided. 'Hugh wants to talk to Mr Brock.'

The man stood up. 'It's Bill,' he glanced at her left hand, 'Mrs Duncan.'

'I hope you enjoy your stay in the Highlands,' Elizabeth said. 'How do you know Lady. Annabel?'

'I didn't, until earlier this week. A friend does and asked me to join his fishing party.' He smiled down at her. 'You're lucky to live in such a beautiful spot. I've fished all over the place but this beats the band!'

There was a burst of laughter from the direction of the swing boats.

As if the conversation five minutes ago had never happened, Flora tugged at her mother's hand. 'I want to go on the swings.'

'When you're older.' Elizabeth prepared to move away when Libby said, 'Is six older?'

'Not enough.' Elizabeth raised her eyebrows at her daughters. 'No arguing, girls. Come along.'

Bill Brock grinned at her. 'Is thirty-four old enough? How old are you, Hugh?'

Hugh understood what he was getting at. He grinned back. 'May we?' he asked Elizabeth.

As the two men strode off towards the swing boats, the girls capering joyfully beside them, Elizabeth was aware of someone standing beside her. She turned her head. It was Andy Kerr.

'Is that Alec's American nephew?' he asked.

'Yes, and he's just met someone he knows from home. Isn't that extraordinary?' Elizabeth looked over at her daughters, now climbing into each end of a boat, in the safe grip of their escorts.

All four waved at Elizabeth as the boats began to swing.

'They are being spoilt,' she laughed, waving back. 'Don't tell Tibbie!'

As she waited, Elizabeth remembered her plan to push Andy and her sister Crys together. 'Crys will be phoning tonight wanting to hear all about the Show,' she said. 'I think she's wishing now she had come up. She's finally decided she wants nothing more to do with Struan Scott.' She glanced at Andy to see if this was welcome news for him.

'That sounds sensible,' Andy said. His

tone gave nothing away. 'Did you see that Lady Cecily is up?'

Elizabeth had not seen who else was in Lady Annabel's house party, her attention having been taken up by Hugh's friend. 'No,' she said, 'but I knew Lady A was hoping she'd get her to come up this summer, away from the fleshpots of the South of France. She takes her role as older step-sister seriously.'

The girls ran back across the grass, their eyes shining. The men strolled behind them, deep in talk.

Elizabeth introduced Andy to the newcomer then turned to her daughters. 'What do you say to Hugh and Mr — Bill?'

'Thank you,' they chorused.

'I better go,' Bill Brock said. He winked at Libby and Flora. 'Really good to meet you guys. You too, Mrs Duncan.' He held her hand in a warm grip again before turning to Hugh. 'Hugh, my man, can we get together while we're both here?'

'The farm's not on the phone,' Hugh said.

'I'll come and find you. Maybe Lady A will let me use her precious Land Rover. Say, why don't we …?'

They moved out of earshot.

Andy was scanning the Show programme. 'How about candyfloss, then the Young Farmers' tug-of-war?'

Elizabeth shook her head. 'I haven't had a chance to see the animals yet but I'm going to find Tibbie first and leave the girls with her.'

'I'll see you by the pens, then? The judging will be finished in about ten minutes.' Andy stuffed the programme into the pocket of his tweed jacket. 'Rosland's definitely in with a shout for best bull. And I hope Rodney Shaw's there to see him win.'

'If he wins it's thanks to yourself and Tam,' Elizabeth said. 'I'll catch up with you, Andy.'

The walk towards the WRI tent took them past the stand. She looked up to see Bill Brock staring in her direction.

28

Peggy popped across the tent to gloat at the produce table again. A first-prize for her raspberry jam, and a second for her rhubarb and ginger!

'Well done, my dear.'

She felt two hands on her shoulders and turned to see her Auntie Mamie beaming at her.

'That's the wild rasps Alec found for me,' Peggy said. 'They were really big and juicy. I'm glad I did them justice. Have you had tea? I was about to.' She looked over to the four-seater table where she'd left Tibbie and Donna. Elizabeth was just walking away, having evidently left her girls with them.

'Tibbie and Donna,' Mamie whispered mischievously. 'How are they getting on?'

'In mutual bewilderment, I think,' Peggy whispered back. 'Look, the table beside them is free.'

Libby and Flora smiled briefly at their Granny Mamie but their attention was on Donna. With her blonde hair, crimson lips and fingernails, and pink frock with its wide skirt, they probably imagined she was one of their dolls come to life, Peggy thought. They sat, one on either side of her, gazing in mute adoration.

Peggy and Mamie parked themselves at the adjacent table and waved to attract the attention of their friend Nancy, from the village shop, who was acting as waitress.

'I've got ever such a lot to tell you,' Peggy said, as cups of tea and a plate of sandwiches and cakes were brought over to them.

'Everything all right?' Mamie glanced at Tibbie, perhaps wondering if they should be including her in their conversation, but she'd got out her knitting — a large brown sock — and was concentrating on counting stitches.

'No. We had awful news in the post yesterday.' Peggy bit gloomily into a ham sandwich. 'An invitation to the gillies' ball.'

194

Mamie laughed in relief. 'That's not awful, Peg! How lovely.'

'It's not,' Peggy said. 'Lady Annabel wants Alec to play the fiddle so she had to ask me as well. What on earth will I wear? Has Elizabeth been invited? I could bear it if she was there too.'

'I expect so, she usually is,' Mamie said. 'But she hasn't gone — you know, since Matthew.'

Peggy put down her sandwich. 'Selfish beast, that's me. I never thought. Well, Alec runs a mile from social occasions but he can hardly say no to this one, so I'll have to put up with it.'

'It will be fine,' Mamie reassured her. 'You know Alec's happy with a fiddle in his hand. And I think Crys will be up around then — maybe she could help you with clothes and things?'

'Oh, would she?' said Peggy, thankfully. 'That's one load off my mind then.'

Mamie deliberated between a meringue and a vanilla slice. 'What else is on your mind, dear?'

Her niece heaved a sigh. 'I told you

Colin seems dead set on finding work on a ranch in California? And now I think Davy's for leaving too.'

'For America?' Mamie stopped, her hand holding the meringue hovering above the plate.

'No, but bad enough. Inverness maybe, or Aberdeen. I found a scrap torn from the *Press & Journal* in his room. It was an advertisement about joining the police.'

'Goodness! What does Alec say about that?'

'I haven't dared tell him. And I haven't said anything to Davy himself. He's not mentioned it to you and Neil has he?'

'Not to me,' Mamie said, 'and Neil hasn't said anything. It's probably a passing fancy, Peg, you know what youngsters are like. Now,' she lowered her voice, 'all set for your first driving lesson next week?'

Peggy gave a mock groan that she turned into a cough when she saw the noise had caught Tibbie's attention. 'As much as I'll ever be.' She raised her voice. 'Tibbie swept the boards as usual in the knitting and sewing, Auntie Mamie.'

Tibbie sniffed but a smile twitched at the corner of her mouth.

'I think I'll go and admire the handicrafts then, if you've finished your tea, Peg,' Mamie said, standing up. 'Goodness, what's happening here?'

Donna had a pretty little bag in front of her, its contents spread out on the table. Lipstick, rouge, powder, and other pots and tubes Peggy didn't recognise. She was pretending to make up the girls, dabbing her fingers gently over their eyes and cheeks. That was nice of her. Even wriggly Flora kept perfectly still.

It was a pity the visitors would be gone by the time of the gillies' ball, Peggy thought, moving her seat to squeeze in beside Tibbie. Perhaps Donna would have given herself a make-up lesson.

In the car-park, the party from Rosland House were preparing to leave, in two big cars. Peggy, about to get into their own old banger, gawped unashamedly. There was Lady Cecily, all grown-up and very pretty. The dark-haired, good-looking man holding the door open for her must be the American, Bill Brock — Hugh had come to find Donna in great excitement and taken her away to see him. And there were Hugh and Donna themselves — invited, because of the mutual acquaintance, for dinner at Lady Annabel's.

'Peg, are you going to stand there all night?' Alec started the engine.

'Sorry.' Peggy climbed in. She patted her husband's arm. He'd had a good day too, having won the sheep-dog trials. With no Hugh and Donna, and the boys staying on in town with their friends, they'd have the house to themselves this evening, she reflected, with guilty satisfaction. Bacon and eggs to celebrate, and she'd open a pot of her prize-winning raspberry jam to have with their bread and butter.

29

Elizabeth pinned Bonny Boy's red rosette above his stall in the byre. He was unaware of his success, of course, but Elizabeth was delighted. If only Matthew could share the moment. But here was Tam, the dairyman, as pleased about it as if Bonny Boy belonged to him.

'It was a grand show, Mrs Duncan. June and Sadie and me had a great time.' He stood, rubbing his nose, his face slightly pink. 'June says she told you about Sadie being adopted? I'm right glad because Isa Robertson's been spreading some lies about it.'

June had not told Isa about Sadie's parentage but Isa never let lack of facts get in the way of a story. Tam stammered over Isa's version of it — *orphanage, Glasgow slums, who knows how she'll turn out?* 'We'd love Sadie as our own wherever she came from,' he finished. 'I can't abide the thought of her being talked about.'

'This time I'm not going to let it go by,' Elizabeth expostulated. 'She upsets everybody, that woman. I'll go and see her this evening.'

'She's away for a few days, visiting her brother apparently,' Tam said. 'It's a relief for June, but she's in a right tizz anyway because we've had a letter from Rita, Sadie's mother. She wants to come and see Sadie before — '

The byre door was pushed open.

'Elizabeth?' It was Lady Annabel. She was followed by a man who had to duck his head coming through the door. 'You met Mr Brock at the Show, I believe. He'd like to see round the farm if you've got time. You're the best person to answer his questions.'

She turned to Tam. 'Congratulations and thank you, Morrison,' she said, nodding her head towards the red rosette. 'I know the part you played in Bonny Boy's recovery. Can I have a word with you about the milk requirements for the House? I've brought a note from cook.'

Tam took off his cap. 'Of course, your Ladyship. Come over to the dairy.'

Elizabeth pushed a strand of hair behind her ears, noticing that her fingers were grimy. She wiped them on her dungarees. Her face was probably grimy too. And undoubtedly she didn't smell too good, having just helped Tam muck out the byre. There was nothing she could do about it. Why would she want to, anyway?

And why would some big noise running a construction company in California want to see a little Scottish farm? She couldn't think of a single thing he might be interested in.

'Mr Brock.' She cleared her throat.

'I told you, it's Bill,' he said, his eyes twinkling. 'How are those little girls of yours?'

'Still talking about the swing boats, thank you. That was kind of you and Hugh.'

'It was a pleasure.' He looked around the byre and then back at her. 'I must say I was surprised when Hugh told me you ran the farm here.'

'Were you? Well, here I am.'

'I didn't mean to be impolite. It's just — the farmers of my acquaintance tend to be rather old and gnarled. And male. And you're not,' he said, in that fascinating drawly voice.

'Give it a few years.' Elizabeth looked away from his blue-gray gaze. 'Well, apart from the male bit. Now, we have arable and we have animals. What would you like to see first?'

He made no move to leave. 'You call this a byre, don't you? I like it. I like everything I've seen on the Rosland estate so far. I'll be carrying lots of good memories back to the States.'

The byre suddenly felt too small for both of them. Elizabeth walked past him to the door. 'We bring the cows back here for milking,' she said, over her shoulder. 'They're in the field the rest of the day. I'll show you.'

Lady Annabel had asked her to give her guest a guided tour of the farm and that's what she would do. That's all there was to it.

'How was school?' Elizabeth dropped a kiss on top of Libby's head. First day back after the summer holidays.

'I'm in Primary 2,' Libby said proudly. 'I've got a new reading book. I'll show you.' She ran to get her schoolbag.

'Any news about the school maybe closing?' Elizabeth asked Tibbie quietly. After a rocky start, her timid elder daughter had settled in well. How would she fare in the bigger school in town if, because of falling numbers, the council decided to close the one in the village?

'I haven't heard.' Tibbie finished a row and put her knitting aside.

She always had a garment of some sort on the go. But this was on four needles and was too big to be anything for the girls.

'What's that you're making?' Elizabeth asked.

'A good pair of socks. I noticed he had holes in his when he took his wellies off. I didn't like to ask if I could darn them so I thought I'd make him a pair.'

'Who? Who had holes?'

If it had been anyone but Tibbie, Elizabeth would have sworn she gave a tiny wink.

'Andy, of course. Who else do you know who needs a woman to look after him?'

'Well, you're just the woman for the socks,' Elizabeth laughed. 'Great minds. I was thinking the same thing, about Andy needing someone to take care of him. I know he's a few years older than Crys but I —'

'*Crys?*' Tibbie grasped Elizabeth's arm. 'Oh, my lassie! Have you not seen it in his eyes? It's you he wants.'

30

'What are you saying? You — of all people.' Elizabeth sank onto the sofa.

'Mummy?' It was Libby, clutching her reading book.

Her granny's voice was unusually soft. 'Get Flora and be good girls and lay the table in the kitchen for me. Your mummy and I will be through in a minute.' She was used to being obeyed and Libby ran off calling for her sister.

Tibbie took Elizabeth's hand in a rare gesture of affection.

'I know we'd both give the world for Matthew to walk through that door, my dear, but it's not going to happen. You're young, you're bonny, you have your life in front of you. Andy Kerr's a good man.'

'I don't — he hasn't — '

'He worships the ground you walk on. Anyone can see that, except you it seems. And he'd be a good father to the girls.'

'But I've never — never thought of him in that way.' As Elizabeth's mind scrolled through the last few weeks her face grew hot as she realised that Andy must have felt she was encouraging him — asking him for meals, confiding in him, making him part of the family. How could she tell him he'd got the wrong end of the stick?

'Think on it.' Tibbie squeezed Elizabeth's hand. 'Sometimes when something's right under your nose you don't see it.'

Elizabeth squeezed back then stood up. 'I can't sit and eat as if we haven't had this conversation. I'm sorry, Tibbie — can you tell the girls I've had to go down to the farm.'

With her thoughts in turmoil she left by the front door rather than the back, which would entail going through the kitchen, and walked rapidly away from the house she'd lived in with Matthew before their short married life came to its strange, sad end. If only she knew more about his last moments — if only she'd been there with him when something caused his horse to shy …

She'd added up all Andy's good points when thinking of him as a potential husband for her sister, but they counted for nothing as she tried to imagine living with him herself.

Of course Matthew had been her first love, their youthful joy in each other deepening as they got married and became parents. That could never be repeated. But lots of people made happy second marriages. And Libby and Flora were used to Andy being around. Tibbie was right; he would be a good father to them.

She wrapped her arms around herself, suddenly feeling cold. Leaving the way she did meant she hadn't grabbed her jacket from the hook in the back lobby, the jacket that had the keys to the farm office in the pocket. She could have gone and sat there until she calmed down.

It was getting too dark to keep walking on the unlit road. As Elizabeth reluctantly turned back she heard a car coming from the direction of Rosland House. She stepped off to the side and stood behind a tree.

Not one but three cars. The house party was evidently having an evening out. The first car was driven by Lady Annabel and beside her, talking animatedly, was Hugh's friend, the American, Bill Brock. The man who'd been nice to her girls at the Show and had shown interest in the farm. In his rightful place as a guest at the big house. A pang of jealousy shot through Elizabeth. How the other half live.

She waited until the tail-lights of the third car had disappeared before she slowly set off for home.

There was no time next morning to dwell on the dream she'd had where she was walking down the aisle not knowing who was waiting for her at the altar. Mr Shaw's bad mood was evident even though Elizabeth couldn't see him. In the office next to hers his voice was raised. She needed to discuss some farm subsidy paperwork with him but it would have to wait.

Now his visitor was actually shouting back. She went to stand by the adjoining wall. Who was having the temerity to argue with the factor?

' ... our agreement ... never thought ... could have been killed ... without a reference ... ' The words banged around the room. She recognised the other voice. It was Frank Robertson's.

There came a crash as if a piece of furniture had been overturned. Elizabeth felt frightened now. Were the two men coming to blows? Perhaps if she got Tam, or one of the other farm workers, together they could try and diffuse the situation.

She tiptoed down the corridor towards the main door. It was standing open as usual and there on the step about to come in was Bill Brock.

'Mrs Duncan, Elizabeth?'

Elizabeth put a finger to her lips. She didn't stop walking until she was outside and a few yards away from the building.

Bill moved towards her and held her

arm. 'What's wrong? You're shaking.'

'I'm not sure what's going on in there,' Elizabeth said. 'Mr Shaw and Frank Robertson, the estate forester, seem to be fighting. I thought I'd get one of the men to come and help.'

'Fighting! What about?'

Elizabeth shook her head. 'No idea. There's always been bad blood between them … But what are you doing here?' She was aware of his hand through the sleeve of her thick jumper.

'I came to say goodbye. I'm leaving for the States this afternoon.'

'Oh.' Well, that was civil of him, but hardly necessary. Their acquaintance had been brief in the extreme.

He let go of her arm and thrust both his hands into his jacket pockets, looking down at the ground, suddenly sounding uncertain. 'I — Annabel told me about your husband. I'm sorry.'

Various possible responses came to Elizabeth's mind but got no further. She opened her mouth but the words, whatever they were going to be, were stuck.

He looked up. 'She's invited me to come back any time I want. May I come and see you when I do?'

Elizabeth's head suddenly cleared. Whatever she thought the thumping of her heart told her when she saw the look in his eyes, it was entirely possible that she was mistaken — entirely *probable* in fact. A rich American, a guest at the House, someone who was on first-name terms with Lady Annabel Mannering, making advances to her? It was a ludicrous notion.

'You'd be welcome to look round the farm any time, of course,' she said, her voice polite but distant.

'That's not what I — ' Bill stopped as Frank hurled himself round the corner and pushed past them.

'Who is that guy?' Bill asked. 'I saw him with Lady Cecily in the garden the other day.'

'That's Frank Robertson. What? Surely not.' He must be mistaken. Lady Annabel would have a fit if it were true.

Elizabeth took a deep breath. At least

there was no fight to break up now. 'I hope you have a good journey back,' she said, maintaining her formal tone.

'Darn it, Elizabeth! I knew the minute I saw you at that fair that —'

'Mrs Duncan?' It was Rodney Shaw's voice. He came round the side of the building. 'There you are. I thought you wanted my assistance with the subsidy forms? I haven't got all morning.'

Elizabeth looked him in the eye. 'I'll be with you shortly.' He stared back for a moment then turned on his heel and went inside.

'Mr Brock.' She concentrated on a spot above his left shoulder — she wasn't going to meet that gaze again. 'I know some Americans like to have a romantic view of Scotland, especially, I imagine, if they're lucky enough to visit somewhere like Rosland House. I'm just part of the scenery. When you're back in California you won't give me a second thought.'

'You sure are wrong about that.' Bill held out his hand but let it fall to his side as Elizabeth walked past him.

Inside, she wanted more than anything in the world to curl up in her own office and weep. She forced herself to gather up the forms and take them to the factor's office. If she concentrated very hard on her work she might forget the last five extraordinary minutes.

31

June read Rita's letter for the umpteenth time. In it, Rita, baby Sadie's birth mother, apologised for the short notice. Her fiancé had been offered a job in the south of England so they were going to get married right away. He was going to drive her up to Rosland on Saturday and she hoped that Tam and June would allow her to make a short visit to see Sadie.

Tam had told June it was entirely up to her — if she didn't want the visit to happen then he would tell Rita not to come. After a sleepless night, June had got up to give Sadie her morning feed. Nodding with tiredness, she went through it all again in her mind.

If she were Rita would she want to see the child who wasn't legally hers anymore? Wouldn't that bring more pain than pleasure? But surely Rita must have thought of that. Could she, June, deny

Rita the sight of her daughter? Was it unreasonable of Rita to ask or would it be unreasonable of June to refuse? Her thoughts went round and round.

But as she lifted the baby over her shoulder to pat her back she thought how little Sadie was yet — the identity of the visitor wouldn't mean anything to her. If she'd been old enough to ask questions that would be different. Of course she'd have to know sometime but ... June carried Sadie through to the kitchen to tell Tam that Rita could see her.

Now that Saturday had come, though, she didn't know how she was going to cope. Fortunately, there was nothing urgent for Tam to do on the farm so he was here with her and he seemed perfectly calm. She could hear him whistling softly on the back step where he was polishing his Sunday shoes.

Sadie was very wide-awake. She looked outside with interest when she was carried over to the window and chuckled when June rapped on the glass to stop the kitten digging in the flowerbed.

June's hand froze in mid-air as a car drew up at the gate.

'Tam. Tam! They're here.' She moved away from the window but not before she saw redheaded Rita stepping out.

She stroked the top of Sadie's head, with its downy soft hair in exactly the same colour.

'You hold her, Tam,' she said. 'I'll go to the door.'

'It was the right thing to do, Junie,' Tam said, giving her a quick kiss. 'I'm sure we won't regret it.'

Tam was right, June thought two hours later. She would have regretted it if she'd said no. The visit must have been extremely difficult for Rita who cuddled her daughter with tears pouring down her cheeks — but it did seem to give her a sense that now she could move on to her new life. When she and her fiancé talked about the town they were going to live in and their plans for the future she became the lively, chatty girl June remembered.

As they said goodbye June felt a wave of real love for the person who had given them their hearts' desire, and on impulse put her arms round Rita and held her close. Rita hugged her back and then with a last look at Sadie she ran down the path.

As the car drove away June felt sadness — and relief. A dark shadow that had hovered at the back of her mind was gone. Now Sadie really and truly belonged to herself and Tam.

'Thank goodness that's over.' Tam lay back in the chair and closed his eyes.

It must have been more difficult for him than June had imagined. She sat down beside him, Sadie on her knee. It would be good to think about something completely different for a change.

'Will you help me with my lines for the play later?' she asked. 'I haven't given them a thought the last few days. The first rehearsal's not far away.'

Tam opened his eyes. 'Good idea.' He spoke in a falsetto voice. "You told me you were broke. Where did the

Rolls-Royce come from?' See? I don't even need the script anymore.'

June reached for a cushion to hit her husband with. 'I hope I sound better than that! I want to do a good job of it — not let Peggy Mackay down.'

'I'll prompt you if you forget your lines,' Tam said, rubbing his head in mock pain.

'No.' It was time, June thought, that she too should move on a little. 'No, I'll go to rehearsals by myself, Tam.'

'You'll be happy leaving Sadie?'

'I can't expect you to come with me every time and it would be better for Sadie to be at home.' She bounced the baby gently up and down. 'With her very own daddy.'

32

The car sputtered to a stop after a few yards.

'See? I can't do it.' Peggy turned to Auntie Mamie who looked pointedly at her watch.

'You've been learning to drive for exactly a minute, Peggy. Was Rome built in a day? No, it wasn't. Now turn off the engine, take a deep breath and start again.'

Peggy did as she was told. It was wonderful of Auntie Mamie to give up her time to such a hopeless cause — how many afternoons would it take before she threw up her hands and declared that Peggy Mackay should never be allowed to sit in a driving seat?

'Relax your hands, dear. The steering wheel isn't going to run away. Good. You're doing fine. Keep your eyes on the road. Mind that sheep. No, it's decided to stay where it is.'

Steadied by her aunt's soothing voice, Peggy was soon delighted to find they were a couple of miles away from where they'd started.

'Pull into this lay-by. We'll stop for a minute. Well done! Did you enjoy that?' Auntie Mamie asked.

'I did,' Peggy said cautiously. 'I might be able to do it — provided you're always sitting beside me.'

Mamie laughed. 'I don't think that will be possible. We'll go on, shall we? I thought the old aerodrome would be a good place to practise turning and parking.'

Turning and parking! That sounded scary.

'How about a sweetie first?' Peggy said, playing for time. 'I've got some butterscotch.' She leaned over to where her bag was, at Mamie's feet. 'Here, have one.'

'So — have Hugh and Donna gone?' Mamie asked, unwrapping the paper.

Peggy nodded. 'Day before yesterday.

Alec was upset, I could tell. The boys too, especially Colin. He's moping about with a long face.'

Mamie raised her eyebrows questioningly.

Peggy knew what she was asking. 'Yes,' she sighed. 'Hugh's going to investigate how easy it will be for Col to get work on a ranch for a few months to see if he likes it, and likes America. With any luck, he'll hate them both.' She smiled ruefully. 'I don't think that will be the case though.'

She sensed a hesitation in her aunt's expression before Mamie said, 'I told Neil what you said about Davey — you know, about you finding the police recruitment article. It turns out he did say something to Neil about it.'

'What?' Peggy held her breath.

'Just general stuff. He asked if Neil thought it would be hard to get in, that kind of thing. And — I don't know if you remember? — an uncle of Neil's was a deputy chief constable somewhere so he knows a bit about it.'

'No! That's all I need,' Peggy said.

'What's Alec going to say? Two sons shipping out. I'll have to get Davey to speak to him. But not until after this beastly gillies' ball — that's, what, three weeks away? Alec will be taken up until then with practising his fiddle tunes.'

'The ball. Well, I have some good news for you on that score,' said Mamie, patting Peggy's knee. 'Elizabeth *is* going. She doesn't want to but the invitation came with a personal note from Lady Annabel saying she hoped Elizabeth would accept.'

Peggy clasped her hands in delight at the thought that her cousin would be at the dreaded ball too — the one held every September in Rosland House to mark the end of the shooting season. 'That's lovely. We can have a laugh.'

'Elizabeth doesn't seem to be laughing much at the moment. I don't know what's up with her,' Mamie said. 'She seems very preoccupied but whatever it is she doesn't want to tell either me or her father. Neil came straight out and asked if anything was wrong but she shrugged him off.'

'I'll see if I can find out,' Peggy said.

'Probably Mr Shaw making her life difficult as usual. Do you know what she's going to wear to the ball?'

'Crys is going to come home that weekend. She says she'll borrow some dresses for you both — can you let me know your measurements? And she'll do your hair and make you up à la London.'

'She'll have her work cut out with me,' Peggy cackled. 'Well, that's the best news I've had in a while. Oh, wait till I tell you what Nancy saw the other day ... '

Auntie Mamie held up her hand. 'Tell me later. Back to the wheel, Peggy! Now, turn on the engine, that's it ... '

Once again Peggy did as she was told. Nancy's startling news, that she had seen a fair-haired girl she was sure was Lady Cecily in the passenger seat of Frank Robertson's truck, would have to wait.

33

Peggy opened Elizabeth's front door. 'Yoohoo!'

Crys hurtled downstairs, although how she could run in those heels Peggy couldn't imagine.

'Come and see the gorgeous dress I've got for you,' she said loudly. Then she put her mouth close to Peggy's ear. 'Elizabeth's in a funny mood. I hope you can jog her out of it. And Libby's got a bit of a temperature. Elizabeth's unhappy about leaving her.'

'She'll be fine with Tibbie, won't she?' Peggy whispered back.

Crys shook her head. 'I'm in charge. Tibbie's gone to her sister's for the weekend. But I think Elizabeth's just looking for an excuse not to go to the ball.'

'She must go,' Peggy said, feeling panicky. Raising her voice she said, 'Let's see this dress then.'

Upstairs, in Elizabeth's bedroom, little Libby and Flora sat wide-eyed on the bed. Around them were strewn open boxes and piles of white tissue paper. On the dressing-table was an array of make-up, enough for a department store.

Elizabeth stood in front of the wardrobe mirror. She wore a full-length dress, with wide shoulder straps and a low neck, in a lovely shade of violet. The colour was perfect with her fair hair and the style complimented her tall, slim figure.

'I've never worn anything like this before,' she said, smiling a welcome at Peggy. 'I don't feel like me at all.'

'You look beeyootiful, Mummy, like a princess,' said Flora.

'You certainly do,' said Peggy. 'Belle of the ball.'

'There will be two belles,' laughed Crys, pushing aside the tissue paper. 'What do you think of this, Peggy?' She held up a dress in glorious amber.

'For me?' Peggy had always loved the colour of autumn leaves. The stiff silk rustled as her cousin handed the dress to her. 'Crys, it's gorgeous. Too good for me.'

'Nonsense. Get out of that old tweed skirt. Your fairy godmother is here.'

As Peggy prepared to disrobe as far as her petticoat Crys unzipped Elizabeth's dress. 'I'll hang this up and do your hair and face. Sit at the dressing-table. Girls, do you want to help? You can pass me the hairpins and those fab sparkly combs. Wait a minute, Peg. I'll give you a hand.'

She manoeuvred the amber dress over Peggy's head. 'It fits perfectly,' she said, with satisfaction, leading Peggy over to the mirror.

Peggy's first instinct, which she hoped didn't show in her face, was to be disappointed. The dress was still gorgeous but she was still Peggy Mackay inside it, with her reddish complexion and untidy hair. But what had she expected? A miracle?

Behind her she could see her cousins. No one would believe they were related to her. It was like comparing racehorses with a Shetland pony. She gave a snort of laughter at the thought.

'What's funny?' asked Crys. 'You look great. And I know just what to do with your hair. Why don't you wear Elizabeth's dressing-gown until I'm ready for you?'

Peggy sat on the bed, her hands clasped round her knees, while Crys swept Elizabeth's hair up into an elegant style. She hadn't realised how glamorous her cousin could look — like Peggy herself, Elizabeth usually wore no make-up and had her hair tied up any-old-how. Her usual garb was old dungarees for working and a skirt and blouse for best.

Looking the way she did now, the men would be flocking round her at the ball. Peggy ran through the neighbourhood's bachelors in her mind. Not many were what you might call eligible, except perhaps for ...

'Is Andy Kerr going tonight?' she asked casually.

She was surprised to see Elizabeth give a start. 'I believe so,' she said.

'Will you dance with him at the ball, Mummy?' asked Libby.

'Don't play with those hairpins, Libby, you're bending them,' Elizabeth said, rather sharply. She looked up to catch Peggy's eye in the mirror. 'How's Alec feeling? Looking forward to tonight?'

'Grumbly, but he'll be fine once he's there,' Peggy said. Hmm. Was there something going on between Elizabeth and the vet? 'He's promised he'll give the car a good clean before he comes to pick us up,' she said. 'We should have a carriage and four white horses of course.'

'Like in stories?' asked Libby who'd come to join her on the bed.

Peggy nodded. 'Like in fairy stories.' Libby was a wee bit hot-looking maybe, now that Peggy saw her close to.

'Oh, Peggy, I should have said. Lady Annabel's insisted on sending a car down for us.' Elizabeth stood up and motioned for her cousin to take her place.

Thank goodness, Peggy thought. Despite her husband's best efforts their car was sure to have lingering traces of farmyard about it. 'I'll tell Alec we've engaged another chauffeur,' she said as she sat down.

Crys put a little cape round Peggy's shoulders. 'Let's see what we can do for you, madam.'

Peggy felt a little breathless as she went to answer Alec's knock at the door. A glance in the hall mirror confirmed what she'd seen upstairs. Not miracles maybe, but Crys had wrought wonders with her little pots of magic and her clever fingers. Perhaps Alec wouldn't even recognise his wife! 'I'm sorry but my cousin and I will be proceeding to the ball in style,' she said, putting on a posh accent.

'What?' Alec looked her up and down bemusedly. 'Is that new?'

'Lady Annabel's arranged a car for us,' Peggy said in her normal voice. 'Crys borrowed the frock. Do you like it?' She twirled around.

There was a spark in Alec's eyes but he made his usual grunt. 'It'll do. I'll see you up at the House then.'

'You certainly will.' Skittishly, Peggy blew

him a kiss as he turned to close the gate.

Alec tipped his cap to her. He was in a good mood!

And there was the car from Rosland House slowing down outside the house

'Elizabeth,' Peggy called. 'Our carriage awaits.'

34

Elizabeth stared out of the car window. Peggy, in the front seat, chatted with one of the estate gardeners who was acting as a driver tonight. Elizabeth hoped that she wouldn't have to join the conversation.

This was so wrong, in so many ways. First, although Libby had waved goodbye with a smile she didn't seem at all herself. Second, Elizabeth hadn't been to a big social occasion since Matthew died. Third, why had Lady Annabel issued what was almost a royal command that she attend? Fourth, how was she going to behave towards Andy?

Since that conversation with her mother-in-law almost three weeks ago she'd tried to avoid Andy as much as possible, getting Tam to accompany him if he was at the farm on veterinary business, and making sure they were never alone when he came to the house to do chores for Tibbie.

Maybe that had been the wrong thing to do. She could hardly avoid him forever. Did she want to? She realised she missed his company, his practical good sense, their reminiscences about their shared history. She thought of his enjoyment of the family life at her house, his easy way with Tibbie and the girls. They would all be pleased if ...

'Elizabeth! We're here.'

Peggy had turned round to look at her. 'Are you all right?'

'Yes, of course,' Elizabeth said, trying to smile.

'Listen,' said Peggy, cocking her head. 'There's a piper at the door. And it's the front door for us tonight, not the tradesmen's entrance.'

Divested of their warm wraps, they made their way into the ballroom, Peggy squeaking with pleasure at the grandeur of it all.

Alec made his way towards them, his face animated. 'Peg, d'you remember that accordionist chap we met in the summer? He's here, with his wife. Come and say hello.'

'But …' Peggy looked at Alec's hand on her arm and then at Elizabeth.

'Go,' Elizabeth said, laughing. 'Go! I'll be fine.' She turned to find her employer beside her, in dark green with a tartan sash.

'What a wonderful dress.' Lady Annabel came closer so that she could speak quietly. 'Elizabeth, I may have done something unforgivable but I assure you it was with the best of intentions.'

What on earth could she mean?

Lady Annabel looked toward the ballroom door. Coming through it was Bill Brock.

'He asked if he could come back for the ball.' Lady Annabel spoke rapidly. 'And he said he hoped very much that you would be here.'

'No,' Elizabeth said. 'No. You had no right …' She looked down to the other end of the room. To leave it the way she came in would mean passing him. There must be more than one exit.

She couldn't see another door but there was Andy Kerr appearing like a lifeboat on a stormy sea. She plunged towards him and saw his face light up.

An hour later she felt exhilarated — the music had a buoying effect and it was hard not to smile amid all the high spirits. But she also felt physically exhausted — she hadn't danced for such a long time and doing so in unaccustomed high heels made her feet ache — and even more uncomfortable about the unfair encouragement she must be giving to Andy since she literally threw herself at him earlier.

Unfair, because when they danced he could have been anybody. She willed herself to thrill at the admiration in his eyes, the warmth of his arm around her waist, the clasp of his hand, but she felt nothing. Nothing at all.

The American seemed to be enjoying himself. It was evident he had never done

Scottish dancing before but his various partners pushed and pulled him into position with much laughter. When their eyes chanced to meet she looked quickly away.

'I hope you'll come into supper with me.' Andy held on to her when the music stopped. 'It's always a grand spread.'

'That would be nice,' Elizabeth said mechanically. What else could she say? 'When do we break to eat?' The sooner this evening was over the better.

Andy looked at his watch. 'Another half hour probably. There's a *ceilidh* part now — I'm singing for my supper! Alec's playing for me.'

Elizabeth remembered that Andy was an accomplished singer. 'That's lovely.'

He gave her a shy grin before releasing her. 'The song's for you,' he said, and made his way to the dais.

Lady Annabel materialised beside her. 'Elizabeth, can you come through to the hall?' Her voice was very kind and Elizabeth, at first suspecting that this was something to do with Bill Brock, realised that something was far wrong. 'Your sister is on the phone. I'm afraid one of your little girls is unwell.'

She led the way, Elizabeth almost running behind her.

'Crys?'

'It's Libby,' Crys said. 'Her left ear's burning red and — listen, you can hear her crying.'

The sound chilled Elizabeth's blood.

'I phoned Mum,' Crys said. 'She said I must get the — the doctor. He's on his way.'

That must have been an ordeal for Crys on top of her concern for Libby, having to phone her ex-boyfriend Dr Struan Scott.

'I'll get someone to drive me.' Elizabeth replaced the receiver. But who? Alec and Andy were entertaining the crowd.

'What can I do to help?' her employer asked gently.

'I must get home at once. The doctor's on his way.'

At the far side of the ballroom, in his strong baritone, Andy began the second verse of Robert Burns' love song: *So fair art thou, my bonnie lass; So deep in love am I.*

Words meant for her. She felt sick.

'I'll take you down myself,' Lady Annabel said.

'You can't leave your guests,' Elizabeth protested, but feebly.

'Is there a problem?' Bill Brock came and stood beside their hostess.

Lady Annabel explained briefly.

'I'll drive you,' Bill said.

'Is that alright with you, Elizabeth?' Lady Annabel didn't wait for her answer. 'I'll take the Land Rover round to the front and then I'll tell your cousin where you've gone.'

Elizabeth glanced up at Bill. His blue-gray eyes were soft with concern. The very last thing she wanted was to be in his company, to be beholden to him. But the first, the only, thing she wanted was to get home to her precious daughter.

Wordlessly, she followed him down the steps into the night.

35

Elizabeth wasn't allowed to accompany Libby into the children's ward but fortunately the little girl was almost asleep when she was led through by a kindly nurse.

Mastoiditis. The hospital doctor had confirmed the GP's diagnosis. An acute ear infection, but the doctor hoped surgery wouldn't be required. They would keep Libby in however to see how she responded to treatment.

The last few hours were a blur. Elizabeth could hardly remember being driven home from Rosland House by Bill Brock, only Crys' white face as she opened the front door. Dr Struan Scott had phoned ahead to the hospital and then taken Elizabeth and Libby in, a nightmare journey with the child screaming in the back of the car and her mother unable to comfort her.

Now Elizabeth looked in the mirror in the Ladies' and gave a hysterical laugh. The eye make-up carefully applied by Crys made her look like a panda now. The hair-do remained upright, thanks to lashings of spray, but lurched to one side. And the beautiful violet dress was rumpled and stained.

She cleaned her face as best she could with a scrap of soap and the roller towel, and then wondered what she should do.

Here she was in town with no means of getting back to the farm — Dr Scott had had to dash off once he'd seen them into the hospital. She'd grabbed a jacket before she left home but there was nothing in the pockets. She would have to borrow some pennies from a nurse and use the public phone in the hospital foyer to call her father.

The first nurse she saw was one who'd dealt with Libby. 'I'd be happy to let you use the phone in the office,' she said, 'but a gentleman was asking about you. He's waiting at the front door.'

Elizabeth heaved a sigh of relief. Her

parents must have hot-footed it over to her house and then, having heard the news from Crys, Dad had come to collect her.

But as she made her way down the corridor she knew it wasn't her dad. She could see the estate Land Rover in the car park and a tall figure by the door.

She was too wrung-out to protest at Bill Brock's arm placed lightly around her shoulders as they made for the vehicle but shrugged off his helping hand as she climbed in — not so easy in her dress and heels. He put the key in the ignition but didn't turn on the engine.

'She's gonna be OK?'

Elizabeth nodded, afraid she'd cry if she talked about Libby.

He seemed to understand. 'Good to hear,' he said.

Elizabeth found her voice. 'Thank you for coming for me.'

'Your sister asked if I would. She tried to phone your parents but they must have already left for your house. They'll be there now.'

So it was Crys' idea. 'Well, thank you anyway.'

'Obviously I'd rather be anywhere else but here with you, on our own, for the first time.'

What? She looked at him, silhouetted in a sliver of moonlight, inches away from her, big, warm, masculine.

'I — I must get home.'

'The guy you were dancing with at the ball — he your boyfriend?'

Elizabeth remembered her lack of response to Andy's touch and involuntarily shook her head. Then, out of loyalty to her childhood friend, she said, 'It's none of your business.'

'Can I tell you something?' He looked away from her, leaned his elbows on the steering wheel and stared out into the darkness. 'My dad had a farm on the Great Plains in the 1930s. Wrong place, wrong time. He lost everything — everything. We headed for California when I was four, with only the clothes on our backs and a broken-down car.'

'That must have been very hard.'

Elizabeth recalled reading somewhere about the winds that had blown away the farmlands' parched topsoil.

'It was. But my dad made good. The American dream. Started the business I run today.'

'I didn't know.'

'I'm telling you to show you that we come from the same roots, farming roots. I might be a long way from the Dustbowl now but I'll never forget it.' He turned towards her. 'So, if that guy's not in the picture, there's no reason why we — why you and I can't —'

'There's every reason!'

'How do you know what I was going to say, lovely Elizabeth?' His voice was gently teasing. 'I'm sorry. I know it's been a very difficult evening for you. I'll take you home.'

He didn't speak again until he stopped the Land Rover by the farmhouse. Her father's car was parked outside and the light was on in the sitting room. Crys and Mum and Dad would be waiting for her, desperate for news.

'I'm here until next Thursday. I know your time and thoughts will be occupied with Libby but I hope I'll be able to see you. I warn you, I'm persistent! I won't give up.'

'But — but we hardly know each other.' Elizabeth's head swam. Matthew, the girls, her family, the farm. Andy. 'I don't know what you want from me.'

'I think you do. But I'll tell you properly when you're not upset.' He leaned across. 'As for not knowing each other,' he said, 'we could start now.'

Before she could stop him he pulled her close and kissed her, and before she could stop herself she put her arm round his neck and kissed him back.

36

They were all in the sitting room — not just Crys and their parents, but Alec and Peggy too. And Andy.

Mamie rushed to envelop her in a hug. 'How's Libby? You're shaking, darling. Come and sit down.'

Elizabeth allowed her mother to lead her to an armchair. She sank onto it and kicked off her shoes.

'She's got mastoiditis.' There was a collective anxious gasp. 'But it's not bad enough to need an operation. The nurse said to phone in the morning.'

'The poor wee poppet,' Mamie said, tears in her eyes. 'And look at you, still in your finery. Do you want to get out of that dress and Crys will make you tea, cocoa — what would you like?'

I would like, Elizabeth thought, to crawl off to bed without saying another word. But of course she couldn't do that.

Changed into slacks, a jumper and her comfy old slippers, she answered her family's questions about Libby while she sipped an unwanted cup of cocoa.

'I couldn't believe it, when Her Ladyship told me,' Peggy exclaimed. 'Neither could Alec or Andy.'

'I wish you'd come to tell me.' Andy spoke directly to her for the first time. 'I'd have taken you to hospital and waited with you.'

Elizabeth forced herself to sound normal and smile across the room at him. 'I know you would,' she said. 'It was bad timing. I'm sorry you all had your evening disrupted.'

In the middle of their protests Elizabeth couldn't help giving an enormous yawn.

Mamie stood up. 'Take her up to bed, Crys. She's worn out.'

'Elizabeth.' Her shoulder was being shaken gently and she felt as though she were coming up from the bottom of a well.

'Crys! What time is it?'

Her sister perched on the bedside. 'Nine o' clock.' She ignored Elizabeth's expostulations. 'Mum said I had to let you sleep in. And Lady A phoned and said the same thing.'

'Libby!' Elizabeth pushed the bed-clothes aside.

'I phoned the hospital,' Crys said calmly. 'She had a good night and they're pleased with her. You can see her at visiting time between two and three.'

'Oh, thank goodness.' Elizabeth sank back on her pillow. 'Where's Flora?'

'In the kitchen. We've made pancakes.'

'You've been brilliant, Crys.' As all the events of the previous evening came to her, Elizabeth wondered fleetingly if she should confide in her sister. After all, Crys had had various boyfriends, was more experienced in handling relationships. For Elizabeth there had only ever been Matthew. What would Crys advise her to do?

Instead, she said, 'What was it like, seeing Struan Scott last night?'

Crys shrugged. 'A bit of a pang, but

I'm over it. Really. And he was in full professional mode. It was fine.' She stood up. 'I put the water-heater on an hour ago. Why don't you have a bath and wash your hair and then come down for breakfast — if Flora has left you any.'

'I'll do that. Oh, Crys, I'm sorry about the dress. Is it beyond redemption?'

''Course not. Ever heard of dry-cleaning? Don't worry about it.' At the door she turned back. 'He's nice, isn't he, the American? Put Andy Kerr's nose out of joint though.'

'What?' Elizabeth felt colour rise up in her face. She bent over, ostensibly to fish her slippers from under the bed.

Crys raised her eyebrows exaggeratedly. 'You can tell me all later, Lizzie Duncan. No secrets between sisters, eh?'

Leaving Crys making a ball gown for Flora's doll, Elizabeth walked down to the farm office. Three hours until she need start for town and the hospital. She didn't usually go into the farm office on a Sunday but she needed something mundane to occupy her mind.

Lady Annabel was sitting behind Elizabeth's desk. What was she doing here?

'I didn't expect to see you, Elizabeth — I told your sister you must take time off until your daughter is better. How is she?'

Elizabeth told her. 'I need to keep busy. I'm going to look at the paperwork on the pickers for last year's potato harvest. It's that time of year again.'

Her employer nodded. 'May I ask you something?'

Something must have shown in Elizabeth's face because Lady Annabel said quickly, 'It's not about Mr Brock.' She put her elbows on the desk and rested her chin on her hands. 'I've heard stories I don't like over the years, about Rodney Shaw — this time, about bad feeling between him and Frank Robertson. Do you know anything about it?'

There was bad feeling between the estate factor and all the employees including Elizabeth herself but she didn't want to be telling tales. Rodney Shaw had been with the estate much longer than she had.

'There was something a few weeks ago,' she said reluctantly, and she told Lady Annabel about the heated argument she'd overheard. 'But I don't know what it was all about,' she reiterated. 'I didn't — '

'The thing is,' Lady Annabel interrupted. 'You may have heard rumours that I'm putting Rosland up for sale?'

Elizabeth nodded slowly. What was coming next?

'I'm sorry. That must have been very unsettling. I couldn't say anything until everything was confirmed. In fact, I have sold our Irish estates and considerably reduced our lands in England. I intend to spend most of my time here and take a more active interest. Get my hands dirty if you like. It's what I always wanted but my father — well, anyway, I thought I'd make a start here, today. I've got a lot to learn.'

She smiled at Elizabeth. 'I'd very much welcome your help. Tomorrow you can get your staff together and tell them that their jobs are safe. And, between ourselves, I intend to find out what's up with Shaw and Robertson.'

37

Mamie and Neil will probably be over at Elizabeth's, Peggy thought, as she cycled along the back road on Monday. They'd come up to Glenmore Farm the day before, on Sunday evening, to let Peggy and Alec know the good news that Libby would be getting out of hospital in a couple of days. Both Mamie and Peggy had clean forgotten to discuss — out of Alec's earshot of course — whether the driving lesson they'd previously arranged for this morning would go ahead, and as Glenmore wasn't on the phone ...

Smoke was rising from the cottage chimney. Drat! Now the arrangement would stand.

'Tibbie's coming home today,' Mamie said, ushering Peggy in. 'She'll be putting the house back to apple-pie order! We thought we'd go over after today's hospital visit — only Elizabeth's allowed in to see Libby. Peg, do you mind if we don't have a lesson today? All this has knocked me for six.'

'Of course not, Auntie Mamie.' Guiltily thankful, Peggy sank into a chair. 'I'll just sit down for a minute. I shouldn't be here — we're starting the dipping this morning but of course I couldn't let you know.'

Neil tapped his pipe out on the fireplace. 'Why was Andy at Elizabeth's the other night, Peggy, do you know? Something going on between him and Elizabeth?'

Peggy thought of Elizabeth, dazzling in her borrowed frock, as she ran from the ballroom and the puzzled look on Andy's face as his eyes followed her, the rest of him powerless to do so. 'I think *he's* smitten,' she said. 'Elizabeth, well, they danced together for the first hour but — ' She shrugged her shoulders. It was hard to explain but it hadn't looked to Peggy as if her cousin was smitten too.

'And who's this American fellow who took her home?'

'He's the one who knows Alec's cousin,

Hugh, remember, Uncle Neil? He happened to be standing near Lady A when Crys phoned, I think that's how he got involved.'

'I've known Andy all his life,' Neil said. 'If Elizabeth's looking for another man he'd be my pick.'

'I hope you'll give Elizabeth a say in the matter,' Mamie said, tartly for her.

Her beloved aunt and uncle were both looking rather strained, Peggy thought, so she set herself to talk of other things.

'You'll have something to eat with us, Peggy?' Mamie said at twelve o' clock.

Peggy jumped up. 'Goodness. No thanks. I must get back. All hands on deck.' She should have left ages ago.

Why on earth had she and Auntie Mamie thought Monday morning would be a good day for a driving lesson, Peggy fumed, as she pedalled hard.

She'd got her house chores done extra early — washing hung out, breakfast dishes washed, pot of soup and sandwiches prepared — when Alec had told her she'd be required to help with the sheep. He hadn't been best pleased when she said she had to see Mamie.

Halfway home the front tyre went flat. No mending kit with her of course. It was after one when she wearily parked the bike and made her way to the sheep fank.

Alec hauled a sheep out of the dipper. 'What the blazes are you up to, Peg, swapping recipes with Mamie when you're needed here? Go and help Col — hold that gate.'

'I had a puncture — ' Peggy began, but Alec was in no mood to hear excuses.

The next few hours passed in a blur of opening and shutting gates to keep in or keep out their woolly flock. At least she could do that. She wasn't completely useless —

'Peg! I said keep that one in.' Alec looked at her in exasperation as a sheep seized a chance to dart out of the pen and escape up the hillside.

Peggy burst into noisy tears.

It was so unlike her that her husband and sons gaped.

'Not recipes. Mamie's teaching me to

drive,' she gulped. Well, that had been the intention when Peggy left home this morning. 'Why can't we have the phone and … ' Suddenly all her worries tumbled out. 'And Col's going away and Davy's thinking of … '

'Mum, don't say it!' Davy's voice was agonised. 'How did you know?'

'Know what?' Alec's bark was gone. He sounded bewildered. 'And you're learning to drive? Why Mamie? I'd have taken you out.'

Peggy fumbled for a hanky. 'I don't think that would have worked.'

Alec gave a reluctant smile. 'Aye, right enough. It's brave of you to have a go at it, Peg. It 'ud be a big help, having another driver. What's all this other stuff — a phone, the lads?' He held up his hand. 'Don't tell me now. Let's get this lot finished. It seems I've no idea what's happening under my own roof.'

38

Elizabeth had wondered if Andy would come over on Sunday — dreading the thought, or at least half-dreading it because part of her wanted things brought out into the open. But he hadn't. As she came near his house on the way back from the hospital on Monday afternoon she saw his car parked outside.

Should she get it over with? But what would she say? Hey, Andy, sorry if I gave you the wrong idea. Actually, I was trying to get you and Crys together. And when I danced with you I was trying to avoid someone else.

Someone who's cracked my heart open with a sledge-hammer. Someone I must forget about.

Oh no — Andy had come out, carrying his vet's bag. She'd have to stop.

He came over and she wound down the window. 'How's Libby?'

'Doing well. We'll get her home tomorrow.'

'Good.'

There was a pause.

'Do you have a minute to come in?'

Inside, Andy took off his tweed cap and twisted it in his hands.

'Have you got a call to go to?' Elizabeth asked to break the silence.

'It can wait.' He put the cap down. 'We've been pals for a long time, you and me, haven't we, Elizabeth? And I thought you were the bonniest girl about the place. I wish I'd told you that before Matthew came on the scene.'

'Andy.' Elizabeth couldn't bear the anguish in his eyes.

'Let me say it now I've started. The last few weeks — I thought after two years you were, well, not forgetting Matthew of course, but maybe ready to — I was going to speak on Saturday at the ball, tell you —'

'Andy.' Elizabeth said again.

'You've always been the only girl for me. But when we danced — I didn't think you felt the same way. I'd love to be wrong about that.' He held her gaze until she looked away.

'I'm sorry, Andy, so sorry.' Looking at his face go pale under its ruddy complexion she hated herself. This is what her well-intentioned scheming had done.

Andy tried to smile. 'Bad timing again, that's my problem, I think.' He put his cap back on. 'Still pals though?'

'Of course. Always.' One day, she hoped, he'd find with some other woman the happiness he deserved.

Driving past the farm cottages Elizabeth was startled to see June Morrison by her gate, Sadie in one arm and the other round Isa who was doubled over.

She pulled over quickly. 'What's wrong? Is Isa ill?'

'Oh Mrs Duncan, something awful's happened,' June said. 'Frank left Isa a note to say he was going off with Lady Cecily!'

'The hussy!' Isa straightened up. Her eyes were red. 'She's led my Frank astray.

The South of France? What will he do there?'

Elizabeth tried to take it in. Frank Robertson, the estate forester, had run away with Lady Annabel's young half-sister!

'What a shock for you, Isa,' she said. 'June, could you make Isa a cup of tea with plenty of sugar? I'll see if I can find out more.'

In Elizabeth's house someone else was weeping.

'Tibbie! What's happened?' Elizabeth went over to her mother-in-law, thoroughly alarmed.

'Frank Robertson.'

'I've heard the news but ... ' Why would it affect Tibbie?

Tibbie wiped her eyes. She gestured to a piece of paper on the table.

'That was pushed under the door. It wasn't in an envelope. I saw the word 'Matthew'.' Elizabeth picked it up.

Mrs Duncan I'm going away I'm sorry but Mr Shaw asked me to put barbed wire in the bulls field, he paid me, he wanted to make trouble for you. I shouldnt of done it. I did another wrong to you two years ago. I was visiting a married lady and Mr Duncan came to warn me, he said her husband was coming home. My truck wheels threw up gravel it frightened Matthew Duncans horse and he fell off I should of stopped but the husband would of killed me. I'm sorry. Frank Robertson

Elizabeth knelt and put her arms around Tibbie. 'So now we know,' she said, and Tibbie hugged her back. 'Now we know.'

'Where's Crys?' asked Elizabeth.

'Out the back with Flora. I didn't want the bairn to see me like this.'

'Are you all right? I'll have to go and see Lady Annabel.'

Tibbie nodded and sat up straight.

Elizabeth went to the back door. 'I'm going up to the House, Crys. Did Tibbie show you the note? Can you phone Mum and Dad and tell them about it?'

In Rosland House a member of staff took her through to Lady Annabel's study. Her Ladyship was pacing about the room.

'Frank Robertson,' Elizabeth began. 'He —'

'So you've heard,' Lady Annabel said.

Elizabeth put her own concerns aside. 'Yes, I'm sorry, what a worry for you.'

Lady Annabel lifted her hands in despair. 'Foolish, foolish girl.' She gave a grim smile. 'I've sent a telegram to my stepmother. We'll see how far Robertson's charm gets him with her.'

'There's something else.' Elizabeth thrust the crumpled note at her employer and watched her eyes widen with horror.

'I'm so sorry, my dear. What a dreadful thing for you to hear.'

'Yes.' Elizabeth took a deep breath. 'And what he says about Mr Shaw? That explains the argument, doesn't it?'

'Go home, Elizabeth. You should be with your family.' Lady Annabel picked up the phone. 'Leave Shaw to me. I'll keep your note for now, if I may,' she said. 'I will need it as evidence.'

Outside on the driveway Bill Brock was leaning against her car.

'I thought this was yours,' he said, smiling. 'Hey.' He straightened up. 'What's wrong? Is it Libby?'

Elizabeth shook her head.

'Well, something's up. Wanna take a walk and tell me about it?'

'I wouldn't know where to start. Even if I wanted to.' Elizabeth reached for the door handle.

'Give me a chance, Elizabeth, please.' He looked down, scuffing his foot on the ground. 'I never expected when I came on a fishing trip to Scotland that I'd meet the woman of my dreams. But that's what happened.'

Elizabeth let her hand drop, reliving in her mind their kiss in the darkness of the Land Rover.

'Today is a really bad day for this conversation,' she said, turning towards him. 'I don't think I can speak about — about something I found out. But could you ask Lady Annabel? — say I wanted her to tell you?'

'OK,' he said slowly, evidently puzzled as to what Her Ladyship could know about Elizabeth's personal life. 'And then what? Can I meet you somewhere later?'

Elizabeth shook her head. 'My parents will be coming over. And Libby's getting out tomorrow. Wednesday? Although I'll be working.'

'Shall I come to the farm office, about twelve?'

But Mr Shaw will be there. Or maybe he won't, she suddenly thought. He would deny Frank Robertson's story of course but if Lady Annabel chose to believe it Mr Shaw would be out of a job, out of their lives. It was a happy prospect.

Bill was waiting for her answer.

'Twelve, in the office, Wednesday,' she said.

Two days — it seemed a lifetime away.

39

Elizabeth parked outside the station in Inverness. There was half an hour yet — but what if the train had arrived early and she wasn't there to meet him?

'Is the Glasgow train on time?' she asked a railway official who confirmed that it was.

He'd have travelled all the way across America, then to London, Glasgow, Inverness — and next week she and Libby and Flora would be with him, doing the journey in reverse.

Her parents were putting a brave face on it. But there was the possibility — never say never, Crys had said — that she'd be moving back. Robbie MacLean had left London to join his father's accountancy practice in town and Crys found that life down south was not the same without him.

Tibbie was the hardest for the three

of them to leave, woven as she was into the fabric of their everyday lives. But she was being positive too — she'd found herself a small house in the village, next door to Nancy's shop and near the vet's surgery, from where she intended to keep a motherly eye on Andy Kerr.

Elizabeth looked at her watch and at the station clock — surely they must be slow?

Then there were great clouds of steam and the railwayman said, Glasgow train, madam, and two minutes later there he was, swinging her off her feet, covering her face with kisses. Behind him came his mother and sister who'd represent his family at the wedding.

'I can relax now,' Bill said, putting his arms behind his head. 'No cancelled flights or stormy weather can stop me making Elizabeth Duncan my wife the day after tomorrow.'

In the rear-view mirror Elizabeth saw his mother smiling at the remark. It looked as if, on their very short acquaintance, she approved of her daughter-in-law-to-be.

'Tell me all the news,' Bill said. 'Has Annabel found a replacement for you?'

Elizabeth nodded. 'Yes, and someone to help her with the factoring part-time. And of course there's a new forester too. It's all change at Rosland.'

A forester with five children, which was good news as it meant the numbers in the village school would be increased by enough to keep it open for now. And the forester's wife and June Morrison were getting on like a house on fire, Tam reported.

Bill and his family were staying with Lady Annabel. Staff took the suitcases and said Her Ladyship was waiting to welcome her guests.

'I want to stretch my legs,' Bill said. 'I've been all cramped up for twenty-four hours.' He held out his hand. 'Let's take a walk.'

Elizabeth remembered the last occasion he'd said that, that miserable day when she'd got Frank Robertson's note, and hurt her oldest friend.

This time she joyfully accepted his invitation.

'I wanna see my soon-to-be-daughters. And,' he grinned, 'I'd like to visit the farm office. For old time's sake.'

'This room is special to me,' he said, holding her tight in the cubbyhole office that, as from the end of today, would no longer be hers.

Her heart racing, Elizabeth recalled the day six months ago when he appeared in the office doorway. She'd resolved to be calm and collected but when she stood up behind her desk she felt her knees buckle.

'It's been a very long two days.' He came forward, his presence filling the whole room.

All she could do was nod.

'I spoke to Annabel and she told me your story,' he said. 'You've had a real tough time.' He leaned over to touch her face gently. 'I believe I could make you happy, Elizabeth.'

'It's impossible … '

'I can't hear you,' he said, his eyes

mischievous. 'Can you come round this side of the desk?'

I won't let him kiss me, she told herself, but it seemed he had other ideas. She found herself in his arms, her resolutions forgotten.

'Marry me,' he said, his cheek against hers.

He had an answer for all her objections — he'd be delighted to have a ready-made family; his folks would welcome her with open arms and he hoped that would make up a little for leaving her own. If she wanted to work, her managerial skills could be applied in other areas.

'I love you, Elizabeth. If you love me too, that's all that matters,' he said. 'Please say yes.' And she did.

Lady Annabel had insisted on them using a room in Rosland House for the reception, with her cook in charge of the wedding breakfast. Elizabeth wanted only her nearest and dearest to be there, along with Bill's mother and sister of course.

'Who'd have thought we'd be back

here for a wedding party!' Peggy drew up alongside Mamie and Neil. And who'd have thought then that she would be driving her husband and sons anywhere? Alec had encouraged her to go out with Mamie as often as she could and she still cherished the moment when, two months ago, she flourished her pass certificate at him.

She linked arms with her aunt and uncle as they walked up to the House. 'Don't the boys look smart?' She glanced proudly at Colin and Davy, all dressed up for once.

'When is it you're away, Col?' asked Neil.

Colin loosened the knot of his tie. 'End of April, Uncle Neil. A ranch in San Diego County, California,' he said with relish.

Peggy sighed heavily. 'We're both losing children to California, Auntie Mamie. Oh! We had a letter from Hugh — Donna's expecting in the summer.'

'That's nice.' Mamie squeezed Peggy's arm. 'But don't think of it as losing children, Peg. The world's a smaller place than it was. Maybe we could all go out for a visit!'

Alec groaned. 'Don't be putting ideas in her head, Mamie.'

It was a dream to hold onto, though, however unlikely to come true. There was no money to have the telephone put in never mind take a foreign holiday. No money to employ anyone except for casual work to replace Colin. But it would be a few years, Peggy comforted herself, before Davy would leave, before he could apply for the police — with Alec's blessing.

The days of the small farm are numbered, he said, there'll be no living for him here. Whether that was Alec's pessimism or the truth, only time would tell.

But right now, she thought, cheering up, there was her dear cousin Elizabeth's wedding reception to look forward to.

Bill Brock kissed his wife. 'Can you forgive me?' he asked.

'For what?'

'Tearing you away from here.'

Elizabeth looked down the room. Their mothers were deep in conversation. Bill's sister was swinging Libby round and round. Flora had a vol-au-vent in each fist and Tibbie was trying to remove one of them. Colin and Davy were eating their way steadily down the table while their mother stood fondly watching them. Neil and Alec were putting the world to rights. Crys and Robbie sat close together on the window seat.

For a moment, Elizabeth panicked. What had she done? How could she leave them? She turned back to her husband and met his steady, loving gaze.

'Yes,' she said softly, 'I do believe I can.'

We do hope that you have enjoyed reading this large print book.

Did you know that all of our titles are available for purchase?

We publish a wide range of high quality large print books including:
Romances, Mysteries, Classics
General Fiction
Non Fiction and Westerns

Special interest titles available in large print are:
The Little Oxford Dictionary
Music Book, Song Book
Hymn Book, Service Book

Also available from us courtesy of Oxford University Press:
Young Readers' Dictionary
(large print edition)
Young Readers' Thesaurus
(large print edition)

For further information or a free brochure, please contact us at:
Ulverscroft Large Print Books Ltd.,
The Green, Bradgate Road, Anstey,
Leicester, LE7 7FU, England.
Tel: (00 44) **0116 236 4325**
Fax: (00 44) **0116 234 0205**

Other titles in the
Linford Romance Library:

HEART OF THE MOUNTAIN

Carol MacLean

Emotionally burned out from her job as a nurse, Beth leaves London for the Scottish Highlands and the peace of her aunt's cottage. Here she meets Alex, a man who is determined to live life to the full after the death of his fiancée in a climbing accident. Despite her wish for a quiet life, Beth is pulled into a friendship with Alex's sister, bubbly Sarah-Jayne, and finds herself increasingly drawn to Alex . . .

MIDSUMMER MAGIC

Julie Coffin

Fearing that her ex-husband plans to take their daughter away with him to New Zealand, Lauren escapes with little Amy to the remote Cornish cottage bequeathed to her by her Great-aunt Hilda. But Lauren had not even been aware of Hilda's existence until now, so why was the house left to her and not local schoolteacher Adam Poldean, who seemed to be Hilda's only friend? Lauren sets out to learn the answers — and finds herself becoming attracted to the handsome Adam as well.